A
PEARL
FROM MY
RIBS

SIMILOLUWA OLUSHOLA

A Pearl From My Ribs

Published by Cornerstone Publishing

A Division of Cornerstone Creativity Group LLC
Info@thecornerstonepublishers.com
www.thecornerstonepublishers.com

Author's Contact

To book the author to speak at your next event or to order bulk copies of this book, please, use the information below:

simi.olushola01@gmail.com

Printed in the United States of America.

DEDICATION

To

Olakunle *mi,*

The husband of my youth and my forever friend,

On the occasion of our 20th wedding anniversary,

I love life with you.

I would do it again, all over again, if life brought me back to your arms.

The first twenty years have gone blissfully, by God's grace

the next many decades will be filled with even more fun and love ahead.

I love you, my man - Adeorimi, my prayer partner, my calmness.

A Pearl from Your Ribs,

-Similoluwa

CONTENTS

ACKNOWLEDGMENTS

To the livewire of my life: My Father in Heaven, my Savior Jesus, and my best friend forever, the Holy Spirit—thank you for the continued strength, ideas, vision, and help. I am complete in You.

To the husband of my youth, Olakunle, it's easy to write love stories because I live in love and am surrounded by your love. Thank you for encouraging me to write and express my talents. Congratulations on our 20th wedding anniversary—our love will know no bounds, in Jesus' name. Amen.

I want to specially acknowledge the patience and love of my amazing children during the writing of this book. I love you, Toluwani, Obaloluwa, Okikioluwa, and Apataoluwa. You are trees planted by the rivers of water that bring forth fruit in its season. Your leaves will not wither, and whatever you do shall prosper. I am blessed to be your mom.

To my family and friends, thank you for being part of this journey.

And to all members of RCCG Ark of God, Dallas, Texas, my faith family—you are beyond wonderful.

CHAPTER ONE

If forever was a place,
It would be with you,
Happiness is being with you, joy is laughing and crying
with you.

"Congratulations, my soon-to-be Mrs. Akinja. I look forward to forever with you. – Love, Mr. Akinja." Hazel let out a merry laugh, as she received the exquisite bouquet of flowers from the delivery man. They were white-colored, with fresh green leaves. Green was her favorite color. She smelled the flowers and smiled.

She was staying in a hotel with her close friends. Despite her passionate plea to keep things simple, they had insisted on making the day special. She gently placed the lilies of the valley on the side table, the golden vase glittering in the rays of the morning sun. Today was very significant in her and Richard's lives as they prepared to exchange their vows and seal their relationship forever.

Hazel glanced in the mirror, noting how beautiful she looked. She was thirty-four years old but looked twenty-two. Her lovely and innocent look gave her that advantage. She could easily pass for Miss World, having actually won the Miss Lagos pageant some years ago. She was beauty personified, with a flawless skin and a radiant glow. She was the perfect bride. Her smiles were gracious, her eyes bore into the soul of people. Richard had known he would marry her the moment they met. He had worked so hard to get to this point and nothing would stop this union.

Her phone beeped and she knew it was Richard. He had promised not to talk to her till they saw in church but anticipation had obviously made him unable to keep to the promise. She smiled, as she picked the phone, her heart fluttering.

"Richard...thank you for my flowers."

"My forever beauty queen, my freshness, my lilies, my wife."

Richard had a way with words, always calm but never lacking the right things to say to Hazel.

Hazel laughed lightly, feeling so happy and refreshed. Yet, she couldn't shake off the disbelief that she was going through this again. Her mind briefly wandered from Richard, and she felt a sudden pang of sadness. She remembered Ethan, her husband of one year, who had passed away ten years ago. His death had left a permanent hole in her heart. Hazel thought about him for a moment.

She had tried to move on but thoughts of him always found a way into her heart. She was who she was because of his love and kindness. Her wealth had come through him, and she owed him a great deal. His death was the rudest shock she had ever experienced, leading her to being admitted into a mental health hospital for almost a year for treatment. She had lost her confidence and purpose; Ethan had been everything to her.

Hazel noticed a tear drop and said softly, "That was for you, Ethan. Even though I am moving on today, I will never forget the nicest person I ever met. Be happy for me in heaven. Richard picked me up from the pieces of my life and was able to wait three years for this to happen. I have healed but the scars remain. I wish you had lived longer and not been cut off at your prime, but our God knows best. I move on today, Ethan, but know that I appreciate the years you gave me for our togetherness, both in our courtship and marriage. I pray this works out for Richard and me. May your soul continue to rest in peace, Ethan Adebayo."

"Are you there, Hazel?" Richard asked.

Hazel realized she had not heard a word he said, as she was temporarily lost in her own world.

"Hazel, are you okay?" Richard asked, noticing that his bride-to-be seemed slightly distracted.

"Yes, love," she muttered, feeling slightly guilty.

"FaceTime me now," Richard said, sensing that she was crying.

"Oh, no, Richard; you promised we wouldn't talk till we saw in church but you've called me, and now you want FaceTime," she protested.

"No, I am no longer interested in waiting. I need to see your face." He started the FaceTime call and Hazel quickly wiped her eyes, knowing not to waste his time. Richard wasn't playing.

"Richard, please trust me, I am fine."

"Pick my call, Hazel, or I'll drive over there in 20 minutes."

Hazel knew that wasn't a threat; Richard would never threaten her – but he would do exactly as he had said.

"I am picking up my car keys now, Hazel," he said, grabbing his Maserati car keys from his desk. His determination was evident.

"Oh, no, Richie, I will pick up. Please, don't come."

She switched the call from audio to FaceTime and smiled happily, trying to hide the tears.

"Why are you crying, my love?" Richard asked, scrutinizing every detail of her face.

"You thought about him, right?" Richard said, referring to Ethan.

Hazel nodded. This was one of the reasons she was marrying Richard - he knew her highs and lows.

"I could tell," Richard said softly. "I know it's been tough putting this behind you. I salute your courage to move on. But, my love, Ethan is gone. He wouldn't be happy knowing you've been so sad for so long. Today, sunshine, a new life begins for you, for us. If you feel we should put the wedding on hold, I can call the pastor right away," Richard said, seriously but gently, hoping she wouldn't agree.

"Oh, no!" Hazel dismissed the idea. "How can you say that, my love? You've been the reason I've lived these past three years. I died many times, Richard. I lost my mind; I was shattered. But you picked me up, against your parents' wishes, especially your mom's. I had never felt love in such a simple yet powerful way. You are every woman's dream - my dream, my prayer come true. We are going to church today, and I will be Mrs. Richard Akinja, as you called me a while ago."

A sweet smile crept across her face now, and Richard felt immense relief.

"There goes my princess, my queen, my all. That is the smile that melts my heart. I want you to know I love you, and I will spend my life loving you the more."

"I love you too, Richard. Thank you!"

"So, get dressed now, and look perfect in your wedding gown. I can't wait to kiss my bride."

"I know you've waited to do just more than that." She winked knowingly

"Oh that…" he replied, smiling.

"I will spend my whole life bonding with you and enjoying our great honeymoon. Our lives will be filled with joy and plenty of children from our *'projects'.*"

Hazel laughed, knowing what the word project meant to Richard. She ended the call shortly after that, feeling a renewed zest.

The effect Richard had on her was powerful. He had a strong effect on many women, and he knew it. He was not promiscuous, but every woman wanted Richard at all costs. She wondered why he loved her so much. An heir to a multinational conglomerate, he was born a multi-billionaire. And he chose her. He was so good-looking and kind, but he chose her and made sure everyone knew it was her and her alone.

She stared at her champagne wedding gown; it had cost a whopping $250,000. She could not believe her eyes when it was delivered. Richard had gone to Paris for it and would not hear any of her protests that it was her second marriage and buying expensive things was not necessary. She had begged, argued and tried to return it but he would not allow that. He wanted his bride to be adorned in the most beautiful handcrafted wedding gown, even though the guest list was less than a hundred. Her engagement ring, a pure diamond, had cost $60,000. She could not believe that the expenses for this one-hour ceremony and probably another two-hour reception were over one million dollars!

She knelt down and said her prayers, thankful to God for the 15th of March. It would forever be the most memorable day of her life, the day God was giving her a second chance at love and marriage. Who cared about this widow? This nobody? She knew this was nothing but grace. She got up and soon stepped into the bathroom for her shower. She took her time there, savoring the joy and gladness that enveloped her.

****

The entrance to the church bloomed with live flowers - beautifully decorated - and the ambience was perfect. Everyone marveled at Hazel's handiwork. As an expert decorator and the highly sought-after CEO of Hazy Flowers and Decor, her skills were truly unparalleled. Her decoration of the venue the previous day with the assistance of her employees was top-notch. The carpet, lush and green, had guests thinking it was real grass.

As Hazel stepped into the church, she noticed Richard in front, waiting for her. She ignored the disapproving glances of her would-be in-laws. They never liked her as a choice but that did not matter now. She only looked at her father-in-law who had been supportive from the beginning. Her parents were seated not too far from her in-laws. They smiled when they saw her, sending their love and prayers. She waved back happily. Her parents had seen a bit of a hard life, and she was grateful to be able to care for them.

Her maid of honor walked closely beside her. She recalled how her twin sister, Helen, had played that role eleven years ago, before her tragic death in a motor accident. She prayed that her sister's soul continued to rest in peace. Haven survived so many tragedies, Hazel felt as strong as a horse now.

Finally, she was standing beside Richard Abidemi Akinja. He looked so handsome, so sharp, his cologne filling her senses. Richard glanced at Hazel. She looked ravishing in her wedding gown; her beauty glowed through her veil. She was eager to be joined to her heartthrob. Yet, beneath the excitement, was a twinge of sadness, as she recalled going through a similar experience eleven years ago with Ethan.

Richard gently squeezed Hazel's hand, reassuring her. She smiled through her veil. Richard was arguably the most handsome and caring man she had known since the death of Ethan.

"You seem distracted," Richard whispered. Hazel smiled back. "I am with you now, nothing else matters."

The officiating minister of the ceremony, Pastor Tim, approached them with a smile. He was particularly happy for Hazel. So many men had sought her hand in marriage, and she had turned them down. He was aware of all her life's struggles: the death of her husband and twin sister, her other losses, her tears, fears, doubts, anger, and mental health issues. He had encouraged her relationship with Richard, when they started three years ago, but it had taken her a total of ten years to be ready to marry again.

Pastor Tim had met Hazel some years back when she relocated to Lagos from Abuja and attended his church. Despite the difficulties she faced, she had remained faithful in her service to the Lord as the praise and worship singer. Her voice was always a beautiful highlight of the service.

Today, Hazel planned to surprise Richard with a solo performance at the reception, thanking God for her journey so far. Pastor Tim supported the idea and kept it a secret from Richard. The processional hymn, one of Hazel's favorites, was coming to an end:

I want to scale the utmost height
And catch a gleam of glory bright;
But still I'll pray till rest I've found,
"Lord, lead me on to higher ground."

Lord, lift me up, and let me stand
By faith on heaven's table land
A higher plane than I have found
Lord, plant my feet on higher ground.

After the hymn, Pastor Tim gave an exhortation on the importance of love and unity in marriage, reminding the couple of the blessings and responsibilities of the marital union, as ordained by the Lord. He charged Hazel to be a great wife and submit to Richard, while charging Richard to love and protect Hazel, as Christ does for His church.

It was soon time for the joining of the couple, and Pastor Tim asked both to get up and step forward. He blessed the rings and the Bible on which the rings were placed. He always preferred to use the Bible for the joining and let the couples exchange the rings afterward.

Then came that part no one really liked to hear at their wedding. Pastor Tim cleared his throat. "Does anyone present know of any reason that this couple should not be joined in holy matrimony? Speak now or forever hold your peace."

The room was quiet for the three times he repeated the question.

"I now pronounce you..."

A big uproar erupted at the back. Some people ran towards the exit, unable to believe what they were seeing. Pastor Tim's gaze followed their frantic movements. He paused for a moment, trying to make out what was happening. It looked like a military troop. He saw men in uniform with guns slung over their shoulders. There were about fifty of them. In his confusion, he noticed a tall, fine but tired-looking middle-aged man walking steadily towards the altar. Even the ushers could not stop him. He was well built, like he had spent much time in the gym. No one dared to stop him, considering the troop that followed him. All the guests simply moved aside. Those who recognized him almost fainted from shock.

As the man continued his approach, Hazel, whose back was turned to the audience, wondered why Pastor Tim stopped at "I now pronounce you…" She had been eagerly waiting to hear "man and wife", which she completed in her heart. Noticing the astonished gaze of Pastor Tim, she looked back and saw the approaching man. He looked vaguely familiar. His strides were steady and he stared at her knowingly. He was dressed in khaki pants and a dark brown shirt, wearing sunglasses even inside the hall. She noticed that the men behind him were military personnel with guns, carried in a non-threatening manner.

Hazel was confused about the approaching man's identity, so she lifted her veil to have a better view. She froze in disbelief and gasped for air, losing her balance in the process, but was caught by Richard.

Richard stared at the man disrupting the wedding proceedings. The whole crowd was in chaos, reacting to the man's confident strides towards Hazel. As Hazel, now with her veil completely pulled aside, looked intently at the man, the ground under her feet felt like it was spinning. And with another gasp, she fainted.

CHAPTER TWO

The fight for destiny starts at conception.
Classmate does not make grace-mate
Life deals differently with us.

Janet Makinde was resting in bed at the mother and baby unit, after a long and difficult labor. She was delivering a set of twins and had endured twelve grueling hours, during which the Pitocin intravenous (IV) infusion that was meant to induce labor did not work as expected. The doctor had tried and was going to do a caesarian section to save her life and the babies', but then, Janet started to dilate so quickly and was able to push the first baby out. She smiled at the cheers but was encouraged to keep pushing harder. The journey was long and very painful but after another 18 minutes, within the same hour, the second baby arrived.

Exhausted, Janet dozed off under the effects of anesthesia. Henry, thrilled to be the latest dad of twins, could not contain his joy. He took a close look at his identical baby girls, then smiled at Janet and kissed her forehead.

"You did it, honey," Henry said tenderly. Janet, tired and barely conscious, felt her husband's hand holding hers and muttered a faint "Hmmm" before dozing off again.

"Congratulations, Henry! They both look just like their beautiful mom," said Dr. Martins, the attending gynecologist, patting Henry on the shoulder. Henry had arrived a little late for the girls' delivery, barely making it in time for the birth of the second twin. He had returned from a short trip too late to witness the first twin's birth. However, he was thrilled to be allowed in just as the second twin was born.

"Thank you, Dr. Martins," Henry replied, smiling broadly. He looked at his wife, grateful that they finally had their children after waiting for five years. This was Janet's fifth pregnancy; the previous four had ended in miscarriage. Overjoyed, he danced and then called his parents to inform them of the arrival of their granddaughters. They rejoiced and celebrated with him.

As Janet rested, Henry quickly went to his car, recalling that he had left the windows open, and it was getting late. The hospital was situated on a three-acre property. In his euphoria, he noticed a mother walking with her two young daughters, who looked strikingly identical. The girls, who were apparently twins, looked so pretty and Henry was happy because he now had his own girls. One of the girls ran to him and hugged him. Startled but pleased, he hugged her back and smiled at her mother, who was approaching. The little girl was just around five or six years old.

"Hello darling," Henry greeted the little one, bending down to her level. "What's your name?"

"Daniella," she replied, then added, excitedly, "That's my twin sister. Our mommy loves us so much, but I think she loves my sister more." She made a face when she said this, to show that she meant the words. Henry was shocked and at a loss for words. Why would such a young child feel that way? He wanted to probe further but the mother had arrived and taken her hand.

"I am so sorry, my daughter can be quite forward," she apologized.

"It's okay. She says they are twins," Henry remarked, still processing Daniella's comment.

"Yes, Daniella and Deborah," the mother replied.

"How old are they?"

"Five," she answered, holding Daniella's hand firmly.

"They are lovely. God bless them," Henry said, looking at the other twin who was very quiet and seemed shy, compared to the extroverted Daniella.

"Amen," the woman replied, beginning to walk away.

"You know, I just had a set of twins too," Henry shared, surprising himself with the revelation.

The twins' mother turned and smiled at him. "Oh, wow! Congratulations, sir. I guess Daniella could sense that, maybe that's why she came to hug you."

"Sense? I don't understand," Henry replied, puzzled.

"Daniella has a special gift; she discerns things that most people don't. And even though she's young, I've learned to pay attention to what she says. I'm sure she came to hug you because she knew you had twins."

Henry felt a wave of goosebumps run down his spine.

"Quite interesting," he said. He nearly mentioned that Daniella had remarked that her mother seemed to love the other twin more, but decided against it. From what he observed, Deborah, being quiet and likely less troublesome, might naturally attract more of their mother's attention. Daniella, in her young mind, might have interpreted that as her mother loving her sister more.

"They're lovely kids," Henry said instead, turning back to his car. It seemed the twins and their mother had come to visit someone at the same hospital attending to Janet.

Just as he was about to leave, Daniella turned to him and asked, "You also have twins?"

Henry, thinking the conversation was over, had to turn back to face his new friend. He smiled and bent to her level, her small hand still in her mother's.

"Yes," he answered.

"What are their names?"

"We have not named them yet. Their mom and I will figure that part out," Henry replied nicely.

Daniella looked up at him with a smile. "Are they girls?"

Henry nodded, still in awe of this perceptive girl. Her face lit up with the brightest smile.

"I think Hazel and Helen would be good names," she suggested. Henry was stunned. He opened his mouth in surprise, then quickly closed it. He got up and glanced at their mother, who noticed his shocked expression.

"Is everything okay, sir?" she asked.

"Hazel and Helen were the names we planned for our twins," Henry said, still astonished. Daniella clapped in childhood happiness, unaware of the significance of what she had just said. Henry could not shake the feeling that this little girl had some supernatural insight. He wondered what else she might know.

"I warned you," Daniela's mother said with a knowing smile.

"I have a question for you, Daniella" Henry began, intrigued by the young girl. "What else can you tell me about my twins?"

Daniella chuckled, pleased that he was asking her more questions.

"The first one, like Deborah, doesn't talk much. She likes the color green. But the second one loves to cry and talk a lot. She is a little mean, so everyone is going to love the first one more – Hazel, that is." She smiled again, as if the words were coming to her naturally. Then she turned to her mother and hugged her. "Mom, we need to go now. Daddy will be mad at me for talking to a stranger."

Henry was dumbfounded. This girl seemed to know far more than she should. He thought about asking for the mother's phone number, but decided against it. He knew better than to ask a married woman for her personal contact information without a valid reason.

Daniella's mother took her hand and turned to Henry.

"We have to go now, sir. Congratulations again." She moved closer to him and whispered, "Pay attention to what she told you, sir."

As the woman walked away with her girls, Henry nodded and waved goodbye. His heart was pounding, especially after hearing Daniella's words, *"She's a little mean"*. He could not stop thinking about how she knew of the color green and the names. Did this girl have special powers? Was it a God-given gift, or something else? He was confused.

When he got to his car, he decided to call his older brother, Harrison, who was a prophet. He narrated the entire encounter and Harrison calmly responded. "I have encountered such people before. They are rare. Pay attention to all she said. Cancel anything you find disturbing, and cover your children in prayer. Remember she mentioned that the other twin might be loved more? Make sure to show equal love to both of them. We are thankful to God for their arrival."

"Thank you, brother, I was worried," Henry admitted. "By the way, those names - Hazel and Helen - should I still use them?"

"Yes, since you and your wife agreed on them. Don't forget what I told you - keep them in deep prayer. Hazel and Helen are great names. Congratulations, bro. Have you told Dad and Mom yet?" Harrison tried to shift the conversation, knowing this moment would be forever etched in Henry's memory.

The birth of the twins brought so much joy and happiness to the Makinde family. Henry was particularly thrilled and excited to have twins. He recalled the many failed attempts at IVF, the consideration of adoption that never materialized, the countless prayers and fasting and the entire journey to their breakthrough. He was deeply thankful. He took time off work to help his wife navigate early motherhood, especially since they had been blessed with double joy, and their mothers were not around to help.

****

It was a rainy afternoon, and Hazel and Helen were at school, wondering how they would make it home through the stormy downpour. They usually walked home together since they shared the same course and were in the same year. Both were studying Business Administration at the University of Lagos. The sky grew darker, and it seemed like it would take a while for the rain to stop. Helen looked around the campus streets, noticing that not many vehicles were there to pick up students; most students, like them, had to walk home. She was not prepared to get drenched in the rain.

"What are you doing, Helen?" Hazel asked, puzzled by her sister's shifting gaze as she eyed the few incoming cars,

"I'm not getting in this rain" Helen retorted, upset that she had not found a familiar face she could approach. "I'm trying to see if we can get a ride from anyone here."

"Good idea," Hazel agreed, but cautioned, "I haven't seen anyone that we know so far and it might be dangerous just hopping into a ride with an unknown driver."

"If it's coming out of this school, it's not unknown. I'm not getting drenched," Helen repeated. She was fierce for an eighteen-year-old, often acting as the older sister. Although she and Hazel shared a striking resemblance, Helen was a little more restless and always the first to take action. Only those close to them could physically tell the difference. Besides, while Helen was the one always playing pranks, Hazel was the calm one, not given to strife or pretense. That was another way people differentiated them, along with Hazel's more oval face and natural look. Despite both being very beautiful, it was Helen who loved wearing heavy make-up.

Just then, a car pulled up to their department. The driver rolled down his window and asked the two girls for some help.

"Hello, sisters," he began. "I am here to pick up my sister; it's my first time doing this. Do you know which lecture room she will be finishing from? She should be in Business Law right now, according to her last text, but her phone is off now." Helen checked the car first to see if there was space for two more passengers before offering to help. She looked at the driver and was momentarily thrown off balance – this was the most attractive guy she had ever seen. And he looked warm and friendly.

"What's her name?" Helen asked.

"Eniola Adebayo," the driver replied.

Hazel smiled. That was one of her close friends in class, although Eniola wasn't particularly friendly with Helen. Over the years, Hazel had understood that both of them had very different tastes when it came to friends.

"I know her; we call her Enny," Hazel said. For the first time, the young man looked at her and, for a brief second, could not take his eyes off.

21

"I'll go and get her for you," Hazel offered.

She turned and headed back to her hall, where she found Eniola and told her that someone was there to pick her up. Eniola checked her phone and noticed it was dead. She knew her big brother would have called many times.

"Oh, thanks, Hazel! That must be my big brother," she said, hurriedly packing her things. "My phone died due to low battery. Let's give you and your sister a ride home," she offered as they both headed for the vehicle.

Even though Hazel needed the ride, she politely declined. "Oh no, thank you. We don't want to bother you or your brother."

"Please we will take the ride home, Eniola," Helen cut in.

"It's about to pour, Hazel. Come on," Eniola urged.

"I hope my friends can ride with us, bro," Eniola asked as they approached the car. She took the front seat beside her brother, who nodded.

"Thanks," Eniola said.

Helen was more than shocked to see a man this handsome and well-groomed. Not even in movies had she seen anyone this good-looking. She could not take her eyes off him, marveling at how this gorgeous big brother of Eniola did not resemble her simpler self at all.

CHAPTER THREE

Lovingly yours, waiting to make you mine
No force on earth can rip us apart.

Richard was hysterical, watching as his world crumbled around him. He held on to Hazel, as if her life had slipped away. The crowd had fled. Pastor Tim, now at the front aisle, noticed the man approaching but was unsure of his identity. He recalled seeing photos of the man – Ethan, as he was called - with Hazel a few times and, now stunned, he looked on. But Ethan was dead, long dead. Could this be his twin brother? He was confused and startled. He tried to be calm, realizing he was in charge of officiating the ceremony. His eyes locked with Ethan's for a brief second and he noticed a flatness to his countenance – emotionless, as if he were there on a mission.

Richard did not care about Ethan; all he cared about was Hazel, who had fainted at the sight of this man. He knew without being told that it was Ethan, Hazel's supposedly dead husband. He was not sure if this was his ghost, or if someone out there was sponsoring this nonsense at this wedding. Ethan was now much closer, and his pleasant scent filled Richard's nose.

Richard looked up from where he held Hazel and stared straight into Ethan's eyes. They looked at each other for what seemed like eternity. A whirlwind of thoughts ran through Richard's mind. Words failed him as he became suddenly tongue-tied. He shifted his gaze and noticed a battalion of soldiers in the church. He cursed Ethan under his breath for disrupting his wedding to Hazel. He knew not to mess with this imposing figure, whose face betrayed no emotion.

"Who are you"? Richard demanded, his voice thick with anger and anguish.

"Give her to me," Ethan's baritone voice boomed with authority. He stretched out his hand, indicating for Richard to place Hazel into his arms.

"Who the hell are you?" Richard yelled with so much pain.

"I am Ethan Adebayo. Hazel is my legal wife."

Richard's fears were confirmed – this was Ethan!

"No, you died ten years ago and were buried. You are a scam!"

Richard held Hazel closer, lifting her into his arms.

"We are getting married regardless of this stupid show you put on to ruin it," Richard declared. "I love Hazel and will not let her go."

Ethan stared at Richard. His hollow eyes showing nothing but deep, determined sadness.

"Hazel cannot be your wife," Ethan blurted. And, as if acting out a well-rehearsed drama, he quickly pulled up his shirt, revealing a deep scar on the left side of his chest. The scar was ghastly.

"This scar was what kept me going, brother. I have suffered these past ten years because of Hazel. She is not just any woman but my life. You can never marry Hazel; you don't have what it takes to be her husband." He glanced at the almost lifeless body of Hazel in Richard's arms. The tension between the two men was fierce.

Richard looked at Hazel in his arms, his love, his happiness, his life. Hazel looked lifeless and, for a moment that seemed like an eternity, Richard forgot his cardiopulmonary resuscitation (CPR) skills he was taught. He just noticed that her breath was faint.

Ethan moved closer, gazing at Hazel's face – the same face he had seen for the past ten years in his dreams, in mirrors, in his thoughts, and everywhere. He reached out to gently stroke her hand, and instantly, Hazel sneezed repeatedly. Richard felt a wave of relief seeing Hazel come back to life, though he was troubled by how a single touch from Ethan had revived her.

Ethan smiled. Same effect, same result, he thought, recalling how his touch used to arouse Hazel significantly when they were newly married. He watched as Hazel opened her eyes and looked at him. Hazel was horrified at the sight of Ethan and clung tightly to Richard. Richard smiled warmly, embracing her.

"It's okay, sweetheart. I'm here. We've all had a bad dream today," Richard assured her.

Hazel kept clinging to Richard. "Take me out of here, please, honey. This is so scary."

"Absolutely, honey," Richard replied.

Ethan moved closer to them. "Hazel, I came for you. I did not die; I was held captive, and this is not the place or time to tell you everything. I suffered all for you, Hazel. I love you so dearly – I never stopped loving you for these past ten years."

"Ugh?" Hazel groaned. She closed her eyes, inhaling the familiar scent of Richard's perfume, Sauvage Elixir X Baccarat - his favorite, which used to be sold for $8,200. The fragrance was soothing, yet her head throbbed with pain. She could not believe that no one was left at the ceremony. Richard scooped her up in his arms, while Ethan watched, his eyes filled with a mix of longing and sadness. Richard wrapped his arms tightly around his would-be wife, carrying her out of the church. The troops parted to make way for them. Their presence disgusted Richard.

Outside, Richard saw some guests hanging around. The first were Hazel's worried parents, who looked like they had seen a ghost. It felt like a scene from a movie and they feared for their daughter's life. Their friends were worried too; some couldn't understand who this man was. Richard's family, especially his mother, had an "I told you so" look. Others had fled the church in fear when the military arrived. His father and a few close friends were also nearby, all with expressions of confusion and concern.

This was supposed to be a perfect wedding – quiet, yet grand. Richard had spared no expense to make it memorable, but now, he was not in the mood to talk or explain anything to anyone. He made his way to his car and on seeing him, his driver quickly opened the back door. Richard carefully placed Hazel in the back seat and sat beside her.

"Apata General Hospital, fast!" Richard instructed the driver. "We need to get Hazel to the clinic. She looks pale and is in and out of shock."

Hazel closed her eyes again, tears rolling down her cheeks. What was happening to her? Ethan was dead and buried - she performed his rites after the plane crash. The passenger manifest had shown his name. He had boarded the plane from Abuja to Kaduna in Nigeria and it crashed, leaving her devastated. A part of her had died with him. Who was this man claiming to be Ethan? The resemblance was too striking - the voice, the way he spoke, everything was the same.

She wondered what he meant by *"I suffered all for you, Hazel I love you so dearly — I never stopped loving you for these past ten years."* Suffered? Had she heard correctly? Was this truly Ethan Adebayo? She tried to will herself to die but death did not come. Instead, she opened her eyes slightly and found herself gazing into the gentle, worried eyes of Richard Akinja. Her love and the reason for her existence.

Hazel loved life with Richard. He was every girl's dream. He had left all others to be with her, loving her deeply for the past three years. He had stood by her side, doing everything he could to help her move on from her past. She had been a young widow, or so she thought, with a sad life. Just as she was beginning to put the pain of her great loss behind her, Richard appeared. She was not ready for any man when he came. She had considered it impossible for any man to fill the void left by Ethan. But Richard had been patient, incredibly loving, and had done everything to make her his. He had rejuvenated her heart, teaching her to love again.

As she stared fixedly at him with so much love, she realized it was Richard she was truly in love with now. Over time, she had developed a deep affection for him. Richard was unlike any other man - he was her strength, her encourager, her lifeline.

****

Hazel lay in the hospital bed all night, slowly regaining her senses. As she opened her eyes, she saw her mother sleeping in a chair beside her, and Richard, still in his wedding suit, sleeping on the couch. The soreness at the IV site on her left arm reminded her of where she was. Glancing at Richard, her heart swelled with so much love. She was determined to marry him, no matter what had happened.

The clock showed 3 a.m., and Hazel smiled. It was a divine time. She had always woken up to pray from 3 a.m. to 4 a.m., a routine she had kept for over a decade. It was a habit she once shared with Ethan throughout the brief time that they were married. She smiled, knowing God was interested in an appointment with her. But the thought of Ethan brought a brief frown to her face. Mixed feelings swirled within her. How could this be happening? Where had he been these past ten years? Was the plane crash fake? Questions flooded her mind, but she pushed them aside, focusing on her prayers. She softly sang worship songs under her breath, letting the peace of the moment wash over her.

Hazel eventually drifted back to sleep and began to dream. She saw the back of her late sister, Helen. Hazel called out to her but noticed Helen held a small knife. She briefly wondered what her sister was going to do with the knife, but paid it no further attention. She turned her back to her sister and suddenly felt a sharp pain in her back – Helen had stabbed her. As she turned to look again, she saw Ethan appear, ready to pull the knife out. He did, but Hazel fell down, face down.

She woke up with a start. "Oh my God," she whispered, her heart racing. Was that a dream or a trance? The horror of it lingered. Helen had died many years ago and Hazel had never dreamt of her since the accident. She loved her sister dearly and had mourned her loss so deeply. The dream did not make sense; it felt irrelevant. Yet, it left her worried. Hazel prayed for her sister's soul to continue resting in peace and tried to dismiss the dream as a mere figment of her imagination. But Ethan…Could he truly be back? Was he hiding all these years? Why?

She recalled the moment she recognized him at the wedding. The man she had loved all her youth; the man who made her a woman. Ethan! His love had enveloped her mind for many years. She had mourned him for long, until Richard came to her rescue. But Ethan could not be toying with her feelings. She knew him - if he wanted something, he got it.

As she pondered the dream, she reached for her phone on the bedside table. Her mother and Richard were still asleep, obviously worn out from the previous day's trauma. Hazel felt a pang of shame, thinking about the dramatic turn of events at her wedding. She sighed, wondering what the future held. As she unlocked her phone, she was startled by what she saw - disturbing pictures from an unknown sender.

Some of the pictures showed her and Ethan during his proposal, then during their honeymoon in Dubai, and then a recent one of Ethan himself. There was also a message:

"For all of these and much more, I won't let you go. I was taken away from you, Hazel. I never died. It was meant to cause us pain. I waited for ten years before I could escape the dungeon I was placed in, my love. I will tell my story, one step at a time, if you let me. I have never known another woman but you. Hazy, my love, I still love you."

Hazel gasped, the shock causing Richard to wake up. He quickly came to her side, hugging her lightly.

"You okay?" he asked, his voice laced with concern. His exhaustion was evident in his eyes, the trauma of the previous day etched on his face.

Hazel nodded, trying to hide her phone before Richard could see the pictures. She did not want to cause him any more pain. Richard looked deeply into her eyes, fear creeping into his voice.

"Hazel, I hope you still love me?" he asked, his voice trembling.

"I will always love you, Richard" she reassured him, meeting his tired gaze.

"But this supposed Ethan..."

"Shhh...stop," Hazel interrupted, looking away as Richard's words cut through her heart.

"Was that really Ethan?" Richard asked, his voice barely a whisper.

"How do I know, Richard? It's been ten years. Where had he been all these years? What happened? Is someone playing a trick on me?" Hazel's voice broke, as tears streamed down her face. The emotional weight of the situation was overwhelming.

"No, it looks more like a big joke. Where has he been?" Richard held Hazel tightly, as if he feared losing her.

"Ten years! It is too late now. You've moved on; we've moved on. Even if he never died it is too late."

"I can't imagine living without you, Richard," Hazel said, her voice trembling as she clung to him. Richard felt a wave of relief wash over him at her words, her desperation to stay with him giving him hope. He silently prayed that this bond would hold, that Hazel would not allow Ethan back into her life.

"I know, Hazel. We must fight for what we have, for what we have nurtured and are going to build together," Richard said, his voice filled with unshakeable resolve. Hazel couldn't agree more. The love she and Richard had shared over the past three years had been a sweet balm to her soul. As she lay there, memories of how they came to be together flooded back, vivid and tender, like it was just yesterday.

CHAPTER FOUR

The songs of hope; the melody of its feathers,
Hope birthed, hope alive, hope soaring
Singing sweetly; the sun will rise at dawn.

It was a warm Friday evening, and Hazel had gone to the park down the street. One of the therapies she received from Crossroads Hospital was to connect with nature. She loved the gentle breeze. Many times, she would sit in the park and write in her journal, reflecting on nature and the beauty of God's creation. But today, Hazel left her journal at home. Instead, she decided to use her phone to take pictures of butterflies, green grass, the stream, and other serene elements around her.

On the other side of the park, a group of people seemed to be celebrating with music. One of the guests noticed Hazel, finding her peaceful act of taking pictures captivating. She looked beautiful in her simple jeans and T-shirt, and he was instantly attracted to her. He decided to approach her.

"Hello," he said.

Hazel glanced over her shoulder and saw a drop-dead handsome man with a friendly smile. She smiled back but didn't say anything and turned away. She wasn't in the mood to make friends today. The night before, she had a scary dream about Ethan on a plane, and she came to the park to clear her mind. Making new friends was the last thing on her agenda.

"Hello, Miss..." the man continued, not giving up easily. As he got closer, he realized Hazel was even more beautiful up close. She smiled, but her behavior was odd—she turned as if he didn't exist. Hazel went back to the bench where she had been sitting. She wasn't in the mood to talk, especially to a man.

Richard found her behavior puzzling but intriguing. He had never been ignored like this. Thanks to his looks, women usually responded positively when he said hello. As Hazel sat down, Richard decided not to bother her further and returned to the group he was with. He had been invited by his cousin, who was celebrating her birthday with a barbecue in the park. Soon, Richard put the thought of Hazel aside and joined the celebration.

The next morning, as Richard was leaving his cousin's house to head to the airport, he noticed someone jogging down the street. The woman had a well-curved figure and was quite pretty. When he looked closer, he realized it was the same woman from the park! He waved to her, but once again, she acted as though he didn't exist. Determined,

Richard dismissed his Uber and decided to follow her, leaving his luggage on the curb without a second thought.

"Who are you, and why are you following me?" Hazel asked, clearly uncomfortable.

"Oh, so you can talk?" Richard responded, happy to have caught her attention. "Snubbing people isn't a good habit, you know, and I can't be ignored. So, hello again—and good morning."

Hazel was taken aback by his boldness. She was a little unsettled.

"I'm sorry, but it's a dangerous world. I don't know you, and you're in my way," Hazel said, clearly not in the mood for a conversation. She was just enjoying her morning jog.

"My name is Richard," he said, extending his hand. Hazel nodded in acknowledgment but kept jogging. Richard stood there, more intrigued than ever. He called another Uber to head to the airport, but Hazel's face stayed on his mind the whole time.

****

Senator Gandoki Shaibu's daughter was getting married the next Saturday, and he had spared no expense for his only daughter. The wedding venue was transformed into a magical wonderland, and guests were greeted by breathtaking decorations as they entered the reception hall.

The tables were adorned with elegant centerpieces featuring lush floral arrangements in soft pastel colors. Each table had a beautiful runner and delicate candles that added a romantic touch to the atmosphere. The ceiling was draped with twinkling fairy lights, creating a dreamy ambiance. The walls were covered in cascading greenery, and delicate paper lanterns added a whimsical touch to the décor.

The sweetheart table was a sight to behold, with a stunning backdrop of cascading flowers and a canopy of fairy lights. The chairs were adorned with lace sashes and fresh flowers, creating a picture-perfect setting for the newlyweds. Every corner of the venue had been meticulously decorated, from the grand floral arch at the entrance to the dessert table with its display of decadent treats. The overall effect was nothing short of magical.

Richard, the groom's best man, was impressed. He marveled at the decorations while reflecting on how happy he was for his close friend, Emmanuel, whom he had known since university. But then, something—or rather, someone—caught his eye. It was a faintly familiar figure. She looked stunning in her outfit, and several people were talking to her and taking what seemed to be business cards.

Was this the same woman from the park? Richard wondered, confused. He turned to a friend and asked about her.

"Oh, Hazel?" his friend replied. Richard nodded. "She did all this. She's an amazing decorator. We love her!"

Richard was shocked. Hazel looked so radiant and professional. Should he approach her? He wondered, she had ignored him twice already, but this time, he decided to give it one more try.

"Can I get your business card?" Richard asked as he approached Hazel.

Hazel's face lit up with a smile, but it froze when she recognized him. She quickly regained her professional composure.

"Hello, sir," she greeted politely.

"Hello, Hazel," Richard replied with a grin.

"Oh, so you found out my name?" she said, trying to stay professional.

"It's hard not to when you've done such an extraordinary job. These decorations are breathtaking. I'm really impressed," Richard said.

"Thank you," Hazel replied, her smile returning. She was about to leave, but Richard stepped in her path.

"Can I have your business card too? You can't discriminate—you gave one to everyone else," he teased.

Hazel chuckled, finding his humor amusing. She handed him a business card.

"Only business, sir—nothing more," she said.

"Richard," he corrected her. "Cut the 'sir.'"

****

As the days went by, Richard became more fascinated by Hazel than ever. He learned through his inquiries that she was a widow and had lost her husband seven years ago. She wasn't dating and seemed uninterested in men, as many had tried to pursue her without success.

"Don't bother, Richie," a friend warned. "She's a tough one to win over."

Richard didn't mind. He admired Hazel's strength and dedication, and he decided to be patient. He started referring her to his wealthy friends for big decoration contracts, two of which took her to Germany and South Africa. He never pushed her, but his admiration for her only grew with time.

After six months of friendship, Richard finally asked Hazel out to dinner, and to his surprise, she accepted. Sitting across from him at dinner, Hazel realized she was somewhat attracted to him. Richard had been kind, patient, and never overstepped his bounds.

"You look beautiful as always, Hazel," Richard said, interrupting her thoughts.

"Thank you, Richard," she replied, smiling.

As the dinner went on, Richard knew he had to express his feelings. "Hazel, I care about you deeply. From the moment I saw you in the park, I knew you were special. I understand it's hard to start again, but it's been seven years. I love you, Hazel, and I want to be a part of your life."

Hazel was speechless, not sure how to respond. She recalled her parents encouraging her to move on from Ethan, but it was hard to find another man like him. She liked Richard but was also cautious.

"Why would you settle for a widow, Richard?" Hazel asked instead.

"Hazel, life happened to you. You didn't choose to be a widow. I love you for who you are. You're still young and beautiful, and I want to marry you, Hazel. I'm not here to fool around—I'll wait until we're married if that's what you want."

Hazel lowered her gaze, touched by his words. She didn't expect such honor and sincerity.

"Richard, it's been a long time for me. I don't know how you'll cope with my low moments...my somewhat unstable mood swings. They come and go."

"I'll learn, Hazel. I'm willing to be there for you until those low moments disappear. Trust me, please," Richard pleaded.

Hazel looked away, conflicted. "Ethan was everything I wanted in a man, Richard. I haven't met anyone like him since."

"You've met someone now," Richard said gently. "Give me a chance, Hazel. Give love a chance again."

Tears welled up in Hazel's eyes. "Please don't disappoint me, Richard. I've guarded my heart for seven years."

"I will never disappoint you," Richard vowed. "You are real and genuine, and that's all I want. My family will be so happy to meet you."

Hazel smiled, her fear slowly fading. Richard sensed her hesitation and reassured her.

"Do I take your silence as a yes?" Richard asked, smiling.

"Yes, Richard," Hazel finally said.

"I love you, Hazel. My only mission is to make you happy. That's a promise."

He planted a gentle kiss on her cheek, careful to respect his boundaries.

Hazel felt lucky to have met such a kind, patient man. Their relationship grew, and Hazel's heart slowly opened to love again. Richard was true to his word—he made her happiness his priority, and together, they found something beautiful.

But just when Hazel thought her life was finally complete, Ethan—her husband, whom she thought had died—reappeared, turning her world upside down. Hazel wondered if she was dreaming or if this nightmare was real.

CHAPTER FIVE

I found you early, I won't let you go;
I will fight and I will conquer.
The fire of my love is unquenchable.

Ethan paced restlessly in his hotel room. Mission two accomplished, but three more remained. He was glad Hazel had not tied the knot the previous day. He had suffered for her for so long, and he was determined that no man – not even Richard - would have his beloved Hazel. He remembered her beautiful face in the wedding gown, she looked even more gorgeous and ravishing than he had imagined. She was still the wife of his youth, the woman he married when she was twenty-three. They had shared the best of life and love until that fatal day that destiny tore them apart.

He glanced at the envelope on the desk, containing some very confidential information. He smiled and touched it again, as he had done several times before now. With that parcel, half of his problems were solved, he thought. He brought it closer to his bosom. Just then, a call came through his phone and Ethan picked it.

"Hey, boss…" came the voice on the other end.

"Hey," Ethan replied.

"Mission accomplished; evidence delivered. The coast is clear."

Ethan nodded, his breath hitching. For the first time in years, a tear slid down his face.

"Thank you, Jacob. This means a lot to me. I hope it was all natural and you didn't do anything."

"You are too kind and too forgiving. If I were you, I wouldn't care, but just so you're happy, it was all natural - nothing forced. I pray you get your wife back."

"I pray too," Ethan whispered, sliding the lock screen on his phone and sinking into the sofa. He held his chain with its pendant close to his chest, the image of Hazel embedded in his mind. His emotions, usually buried deep, overflowed as he clutched the parcel and the chain, almost as if his life depended on them.

****

Ethan's love for Hazel had blossomed over the four years of their relationship. He had resolved to marry her - there was no stopping him, no turning back. He knew her twin sister, Helen, had an obnoxious behavior and did not love Hazel. However, Hazel was blind to the envy and jealousy in Helen. Many times, Ethan had warned Hazel, carefully and subtly, but she would always dismiss his concerns. The situation reached its peak when Helen started trying to make him sleep with her. Helen was like a reincarnated Jezebel; yet, Hazel, blinded by love, refused to see it.

Ethan was very wealthy, the kind of man every woman dreamed of. He never drove a car that was not custom-built for him since the age of twenty-eight. He was a successful importer and exporter, bringing in machinery for companies and dealing in gold. He was, in fact, a major player in the gold-mining industry. His gold business had been passed down from his grandmother, and he had expanded it by going into mining and extracting raw gold. For this reason, he owned vast acres of land in both rural and urban areas. He was even planning to open a high-end jewelry shop for Hazel when tragedy struck.

Ethan had invested a significant portion of his fortune into making Hazel successful in the decoration industry, using his connection and status to win contracts for her. He would do anything for Hazel. She was simple yet extremely brilliant, and naturally beautiful - make up only served to highlight her beauty.

Hazel often shared everything Ethan did for her with Helen, since she was her only sibling and best friend. But Helen, driven by jealousy, schemed to break their relationship. She envied Hazel for having a man like Ethan, someone she herself desperately wanted. Helen, who had made poor choices in men, was determined to make Ethan fall in love with her.

However, despite Ethan's warnings, Hazel seemed too simple to fathom the many unpardonable acts Helen committed to try to steal Ethan away. Ethan knew Hazel's parents had raised their daughters well. He also knew that Hazel's mother had waited five years to have them, making them priceless. Everyone approved of Ethan and he was happy about that.

One day, after an outing with Hazel, Ethan raised some concerns.

"Hazel," he began.

Hazel smiled back and looked up from the text message on her phone. She had just landed another contract, thanks to Ethan, and she meant to thank him for that shortly.

"I have something to tell you."

Hazel looked at Ethan. They had been dating for years and she loved him deeply.

"You know I love you sincerely and deeply," Ethan continued. "I want you to know that you are the best thing that ever happened to me after my salvation in our Lord Jesus. When we get married, I want us to be committed to each other. No external parties please."

Hazel smiled at Ethan. "I *kinda* know where this is going," she said with wink and a smile. "Trying to keep Helen far away, right?" She could not understand the animosity between her fiancé and her sister. And she was too simple-minded to probe further.

"I don't want any problems, Hazel. I've told you she's made several passes at me and you always brush it off, saying that's just her way of showing she likes me as her future brother-in-law. But I am not comfortable with it."

"Helen got a job at Landmark Airline," Hazel replied. "She is an assistant manager and the pay is great. Helen has done well for herself since school and will be busy focusing on her career. Yes, I know my sister is a flirt, but most of the time, she does it to taunt men. She might have done same to you but trust me she is the nicest person I know. I've told you how she's fought for me in the past. I will keep an eye on her; but she'll be so busy soon that you'll forget about her."

"Oh, wow! Landmark Airline is awesome," Ethan said with a sigh of relief, happy that Helen would be busy now and have less time for foolishness. "I've flown first class with them a couple of times and their customer service is excellent. I hope she stays focused on her career. The other day...."

Hazel raised her hand to stop him. She hated recalling what Ethan had told her Helen did, which Helen denied. Ethan had come to pick her up for shopping, and while waiting for her, Helen had reportedly come out stark naked, trying to seduce him. It had taken all of Ethan's self-control not to give in. This was just one of many attempts Helen had made to get Ethan to sleep with her. The memory of that incident still haunted Ethan.

"I'm sure this is huge for you, Ethan," Helen had said, her voice sultry. "I'm much better endowed than Hazel, and this is what you're missing."

Ethan had been disgusted and realized that he needed to move Hazel out of the house she shared with her sister. He had tried before, but Hazel insisted on moving only after their wedding.

"Sleep with me, and I'll never bother you again," Helen had tempted him. But Ethan didn't look back, refusing to be lured by her nudity. He recalled his stern response.

"Helen, nothing in this world or on this earth will ever make me unfaithful to Hazel. This is worse than Sodom. Please get out of here and put something on. I'll video call her right now. Don't dare me."

Helen had cursed him in frustration. "You bloody bastard, Ethan! I've tried for years to get your attention, and you've always ignored me. If you marry my sister, you won't enjoy her," she had spat.

Ethan had told Hazel about the incident, but she had remained calm, seemingly shocked but not overly concerned. She assured Ethan that she would take care of it. Ethan, however, was worried about Hazel's indifference and could not understand her lack of concern.

Hazel, in her simplicity, had confronted Helen, who flatly denied the accusation.

"He must be crazy. Me? Stripped naked for him? I think your Ethan is not right in the head. I only came to open the door for him, and that's all," Helen had said.

"Oh okay," Hazel replied. "Just don't mess with him, that's all I ask."

"You're stupid for even suggesting that, Hazel. Is it because I live with you? I don't mess with Ethan, and I am NOT interested in him. Don't drag me into this nonsense," Helen had roared.

Not wanting to cause trouble, Hazel had decided to let the matter drop, though she resolved to be more watchful. Over time, nothing seemed to suggest that Helen was behaving inappropriately with Ethan. Hazel knew her sister was streetwise and not one to be easily trusted or corrected. Yet, at this time, they were living together, and Hazel was making enough money to keep both of them comfortable.

The courtship period between Ethan and Hazel began soon after their parents and pastors had been formally informed of their decision to marry. It was the most beautiful time of Ethan's life. Hazel was perfection in beauty and character. The years they had been together felt like eternity to Ethan. This evening, he planned to take her out to dinner, despite her insistence on cooking.

He headed to Hazel's apartment, carrying a bunch of carnations. He rang the bell, and the door swung open to reveal Helen, not Hazel. She smiled at him but it was not a smile he liked. He had often tried to be careful with her.

"Hello, Helen. Please tell Hazel I'll be waiting in the car," Ethan said, turning to leave. He did not want to spend a second more in conversation with Helen.

Helen laughed sarcastically.

"She is not home, Loverboy," she sneered.

Ethan stopped and turned back. "We have dinner tonight. Where did she go?"

"If you come in, I'll tell you."

Ethan was hesitant. He knew Helen had always been trouble.

"No games, Helen. Where is Hazel?" he asked, irritation creeping into his voice.

Helen's countenance changed, her smile turning cold. "Why are you always so rude?" She snapped, nearly shutting the door in his face. But Ethan held it open.

"Where is Hazel?" he asked more firmly as he stepped inside.

Helen's eyes flashed with mischief. "She's out, but I'm here. Why don't you stay a while?"

Ethan's gut churned with unease. He didn't trust Helen, and he did not want to be alone with her. He pulled out his phone and called Hazel instead.

"Where are you, darling? We have a date today."

"Yes, my love. I had to run a quick errand for a customer with last-minute details. I told Helen to make you comfortable. Please wait for me."

"Please hurry, dear," Ethan said, deciding it was best to wait in his car. He went to the door but found it locked. He turned and faced Helen. Her gaze bore into him, her intentions clear.

"Helen, please don't play with me. I need this door opened," he said, trying to remain calm.

Helen did not budge. "I just need your touch, Ethan. Calm down. I promise I won't tell my sister." She laughed wickedly making a move to undress.

"Will you stop that nonsense!" Ethan demanded.

Helen broke into another mocking laughter. "You, stop!" she crooned, as she took off her blouse and flung it off. "Don't be ridiculous. Why do I have to beg for your attention all the time?"

Ethan's patience snapped. He brought out his phone and held it up. "If you don't put on your clothes right now, I'll video call your sister!"

Helen froze, shocked by the threat. He started the video call and Helen had to disappear quickly. Ethan kept the video call with Hazel going, knowing it was his only safeguard against Helen's advances.

CHAPTER SIX

All by myself, alone in the dark,

No light, no hope. I hear my Savior whisper

Even though you walk through the valley of shadow of death,

No evil will befall you; I am with you.

Hazel was discharged from Apata General Hospital after forty-eight hours, following her fainting episode. Although she had regained some strength and felt physically renewed by the medication and rest, her mind was still troubled. She felt Ethan's presence all around her, even though he wasn't physically there. The pictures he had sent to her phone replayed in her mind, reminding her of the deep love they had shared and the great marriage they had before his supposedly sudden death.

Now, Hazel was overwhelmed by the reality of what lay ahead. She feared the mockery she might face, the laughter at her failed wedding, and the judgment from those who knew her as a widow. She wasn't even sure if she could still call herself a widow, yet she still questioned whether the man who had resurfaced was truly her Ethan. She had so many questions. Nothing seemed to add up, and the mental exhaustion was beginning to wear her down, despite her physical rest.

Hazel dreaded the idea of returning to a mental hospital. The last time she was there, after learning of Ethan's death ten years ago, was unbearable. The news of his sudden passing had been beyond devastating for her. It was just about a year after their marriage. When she first heard of the plane crash, knowing her husband had boarded that flight. She remembered the distress following the news, none of his phone lines were reachable, confirming her worst fears. Family and friends had quickly gathered around her. Badly shaken by the unexpected turn of her life, she became like a zombie, unable to speak or care for herself. She fell into a deep depression, and her health deteriorated rapidly as she refused to eat, despite everyone's efforts to persuade her.

Hazel recalled her frequent episodes of psychosis, panic attacks, and nights of severe anxiety. She was almost always on benzodiazepines, nearly turning into an addict. She lost key clients in her business during those hard times and seemed almost beyond redemption. The doctor caring for her eventually referred her to a psychiatric unit for medication and cognitive behavioral therapy. What was expected to be a quick fix, with therapy sessions and medication, turned Hazel into a psychiatric patient for an entire year, during which she was in and out of treatment and inpatient admissions.

Now, with Ethan's return and the ensuing love triangle, she wasn't sure how to move forward. She wanted to hide but knew there was no escape. Determined to take each day calmly and prayerfully, she placed her trust in God, believing her prayers and tears would not be in vain. She recited one of her favorite scriptures, Psalm 16:8: *"I have set the Lord always before me; Because He is at my right hand, I shall not be moved."*

The verse provided her with a sense of comfort, and she repeated it several times to calm herself. It gave her some relief, but it didn't completely stop her mind from wandering back to one of her darkest moments after Ethan's sudden disappearance.

****

The fluorescent lights buzzed overhead as Hazel huddled in the corner of her room in the psych ward. She was still in shock and disbelief over Ethan's death. She had been diagnosed with Post-Traumatic Stress Disorder (PTSD) and Major Depressive Disorder (MDD). Her family got her admitted her to Crossroads Hospital one month after Ethan's passing. She could hear the muffled cries of other patients, their voices echoing down the sterile hallway. The air was thick with the smell of disinfectant, which made her nauseous.

Hazel had been in the psych ward for a week following a suicide attempt. She had hoped that being in a place where she could get professional help would make her feel better, but instead, she felt trapped and alone. Some of the staff seemed indifferent to her suffering, treating her like a burden rather than a person. She was disheartened that psych patients had to endure such treatment alongside their mental illness. But some staff members were wonderful, truly caring, and not just there for the paycheck.

Hazel wondered how she had ended up in a place like this. The pain of Ethan's absence was overwhelming, and the loneliness suffocating. She was numb, refusing to speak to anyone. She had wasted away from neglecting herself and was close to death. Hazel refused to eat or sleep, becoming a shadow of her former self. Her eyes were often bloodshot; it was a deeply traumatic time for her. Twice, she had psychiatric emergencies where she harmed herself, and if not for the timely intervention of the hospital staff, she could have died. That was why her family believed she needed closer observation and monitored therapy.

Hazel seemed to drift in and out of reality, her thoughts disorganized, and her behavior often erratic. Many times, her face remained blank, emotionless. Her medication took time to kick in, and her progress was slow; it took a year for her to stabilize. Her parents, especially her mother, were her most frequent visitors. During one of Mrs. Makinde's visits, she broke down in tears as she stared at Hazel, who sat through the visit without a word or hug. Her gaze was distant.

"Talk to me, darling," Mrs. Makinde pleaded. "We're in this together. Please come out of this darkness." She tried to hug Hazel, but Hazel moved away, her lips trembling uncontrollably.

"You've been here for four months, Hazel. Please come home. All is well. Ethan wouldn't want to see you like this if he were here."

But Hazel still stared blankly, her eyes cold and distant.

"May the Lord heal your mind, restore your peace, and bring light to the darkness around you, in Jesus' name," Mrs. Makinde prayed. She kept her daughter in her prayers, visiting often, holding on to hope for Hazel's full restoration.

"I'll send you daily Bible passages and some songs to help you recover. I love you, darling," Mrs. Makinde said, trying not to break down in front of Hazel before she left.

Hazel was hurting deeply, and her business suffered while she was in the hospital. During her stay, she encountered others with tragic stories. One that stuck with her was a young, beautiful adolescent she met during a counseling session. The girl was five days postpartum and had been admitted for evaluation after killing her newborn baby. She couldn't remember having a baby or what had happened. She had delivered the child in the bathroom, hidden from her father, who found her in a pool of blood after hearing a crash. When the paramedics arrived, they confirmed she had just given birth. Her father was in shock—he hadn't known she was pregnant. When the girl woke up, she had no memory of the baby or its death, and she had been brought to Crossroads for evaluation.

Hazel sometimes felt out of place, hearing such stories while dealing with her own grief. She didn't know whether to feel sad for them, as she was too absorbed in her own struggles.

Her care team was exceptional. They worked together to see to her well-being. She especially liked her psychiatrist, Dr. Sayd, a kind-hearted and patient man who was never judgemental. He had been recruited from a top behavioral health hospital in Sacramento, California, and was dedicated to his patients. Dr. Sayd worked closely with Hazel on her medication and therapy, collaborating with other caregivers to create an individualized care plan. He was there during both of Hazel's psychiatric emergencies, where she needed restraints—both physical and chemical—to calm down. He ensured her treatment covered all aspects of her care, and she had one-on-one supervision to keep her safe.

Hazel often woke from nightmares about Ethan, running to the nurses' station in distress. Most of the nurses were compassionate, redirecting her with care or sitting with her after giving her anti-anxiety medication to calm her. Dr. Sayd led by example, and the staff at Crossroads followed his compassionate approach. A nurse, Leah, was even terminated on the spot for treating Hazel with disdain.

Leah had taken a dislike to Hazel from the moment she arrived, speaking to her in a condescending tone and dismissing her struggles. One day, she roughly grabbed Hazel's arm, causing her to cry out in pain.

"Stop being so dramatic," Leah snapped. "You're just seeking attention, like all the other crazies in here."

Hazel felt tears prick her eyes, helpless and vulnerable. Just then, Dr. Sayd walked into the room and caught Leah treating Hazel without dignity. That was the end of Leah's employment at Crossroads. Hazel was then transferred to the I-Care unit, meant for sensitive psychiatric cases.

That evening, Hazel asked for a sheet of paper. She had never written a romantic poem or letter before, but her emotions poured out as she stained the paper with her tears:

I find myself going through the motions of daily life, but everything feels empty and meaningless without you by my side. The future we planned together seems like a distant dream.

I try to find solace in the memories of our time together, but it only reminds me of what I've lost. The nights are the hardest when the silence echoes your absence.

I know I must find a way forward, to live without you, but the thought of facing the world alone is terrifying. I miss your laughter, your warmth, your presence.

I must navigate this new reality, find strength in my grief,

*and courage in my pain. I know you would want me to be
strong, to find happiness again. But for now, I am lost in the
darkness of my sorrow.*

Your love, Hazel.

As the words sank in, Hazel felt a wave of grief and
heartache. But amidst the pain, she found a small glimmer
of strength from her care team, her family, and her friends.
It was hard, but she knew she had to be strong—for herself
and for them.

Therapy sessions were intense for Hazel, especially
given her racing mind. She recalled her first session. Dr.
Daniel, the therapist, had a concerned look as he addressed
the group. One of the patients, barely audible, said, "I feel
like I'm drowning in a sea of darkness, and I can't find my
way out."

Hazel nodded in agreement, understanding the feeling
all too well. Dr. Daniel gently placed a hand on the patient's
shoulder. "I know it feels overwhelming right now, but I
believe we can work through this together. You are not
alone."

Tears welled in the patient's eyes. "I'm so tired of feeling
this way. I just want it to end."

Dr. Daniel leaned closer, his voice soft and reassuring.
"There is hope. We'll help you see the light at the end of
the tunnel."

As the session continued, the group began to open up, sharing their deepest fears and traumas. Each word spoken lifted a weight off their shoulders, a glimmer of hope breaking through. Hazel, too, felt the weight ease.

When the session ended, the other patients left, but Hazel stayed behind, reflecting on everything. She was still lost in grief, but the support from the group gave her hope. After a year of intermittent hospitalization, she was finally ready to face the challenges of the real world again. She knew a permanent hole would remain in her heart for Ethan Adebayo, but she was on the path to healing.

Hazel finally began to heal when she attended a crusade, where the guest minister preached, sharing a testimony that resonated with her life. It was only then that she started to recover. But just as she was emerging from this painful period, Helen was involved in a ghastly motor accident that claimed her life. This had plunged Hazel into yet another difficult time, but by the grace of God, she managed to pull through.

CHAPTER SEVEN

The scars tell the story words cannot tell
Love has a price sometimes;
The pain of love and the cost to love.

Richard knew better than to think Ethan would back off after what had happened. Ethan's dramatic appearance, complete with military troops that had effectively halted the wedding, made it clear he was not going to give up easily. Richard had to admit that Ethan was handsome, even more so than in the pictures he had seen. He knew Ethan's return would come with a strong determination to win Hazel back, and Richard was not going to lose her to him.

The mystery of Ethan's reappearance, after being declared dead in a plane crash, troubled Richard. He decided to launch an investigation, hiring a high-profile investigator to help him uncover the truth about who Ethan Adebayo really was. He was determined to do everything to ensure Ethan would not win Hazel back. This was his resolution.

He was confident in his own advantages – his wealth and looks –and was encouraged by the fact that Hazel, now out of the hospital, still professed her love for him.

Later that day, Richard thought of Hazel and called her. Hazel, who was on bed rest for a week, as recommended by the doctor, answered with a sleepy voice, still groggy from her medication.

"My love," Richard said softly.

"Hey, Richard," Hazel cooed into the phone. "Are you at the office?"

"Yes, I have to work to provide for my family-to-be," Richard replied, his tone possessive.

"You will make a good husband and a good father," Hazel muttered.

"What are you doing now?" he asked with evident concern.

"I'm thinking of doing some shopping for the Okparas' event."

"No, not now, *hun*. Please, follow the doctor's instructions and let shopping wait until after a week. The Okparas' wedding is still three months away," Richard advised.

"True, but I want everything to be in place, they made a deposit of thirty million naira, and I want to ensure all imports arrive on time, along with the items I'm buying locally."

"Yes, you mentioned it's going to be an all-glass decoration," Richard said, smiling as he recalled her earlier descriptions.

"You seem to know a lot about my decoration business," Hazel teased.

"I've been paying attention," Richard chuckled. "I'm coming over after work to spend some time with you. We still need to plan our wedding. Maybe we'll have it abroad or somewhere secure. I love you, Hazel, and you will be mine - Mrs. Akinja."

"Yes, Richard. I love you too, always," Hazel said, but her voice wavered with uncertainty. "I don't even know if this is right. Am I a widow or a married woman? Sometimes I cry and don't even know who I am anymore. One minute, I feel like a widow who has gone through life; the next, since Ethan came back, I feel like I'm still married to him. And I don't even know if it's really him - I only saw a glimpse of him that day. I hope no one is playing tricks on my mind," she said, tears cascading her face.

"No, Hazel. You are not married anymore. You're not a married woman. Ethan died in a plane crash ten years ago. Even if he survived, he can't just come back after ten years and expect to have you back. You've mourned him and respected his memory. You're a widow, and you need to stop feeling guilty," Richard said, his voice firm yet gentle.

"I wish it were that easy, Richard. I don't know what to think anymore. If it's the Ethan I knew, he won't back off," Hazel said, her voice breaking. "I hope this isn't a setup from the pit of hell."

"Aww, my baby," Richard began, trying to soothe her. "Ethan is a shadow, and he belongs to your past, whether dead or alive. But there's one important question I need to ask." He paused, taking a deep breath before continuing. "Do you still love him or not?"

Hazel let out a heavy sigh. "What kind of question is that?"

"Hazel, do you still love Ethan," Richard pressed.

"He was…my husband. I never stopped loving his memory for who he was," Hazel admitted, her voice trembling with emotion.

"I understand," Richard said quietly, his heart sinking as silence filled the air. Hazel felt a pang of unease at the distance that suddenly seemed to stretch between them.

"Richard?" she whispered through her tears.

"Yes, my love," Richard replied, mustering all the strength he had to respond. In that split second, he felt a disconnect between them that he couldn't ignore.

"I'm sorry for how I've been feeling. I'm so confused. I loved Ethan—he was a good man. I don't understand this, but I'm most certainly confused," Hazel confessed, her tears flowing freely now.

"You have to be strong, Hazel. He will try to win you over, especially after disrupting our wedding. You must make up your mind, my love. You have two determined men fighting for your love, and neither will give up. So, I ask you, Hazel," Richard said, summoning all his strength. He felt that Hazel needed to be resolute and make her choice.

"Do you still love me?" Richard asked the question in a different way now

Hazel cried even harder. "I love you, Richard. Please, help me," she said, her voice choked with tears.

Richard allowed himself a brief smile. "I can't continue at work, Hazel. I'm on my way to your place. My secretary will cancel all my meetings for today," he said with renewed determination, knowing he had to fight for her. He hung up the phone and remembered the task at hand: tracking down Ethan's background. He had the contact of a highly esteemed investigator, known for his discretion and reliability. This was to be kept secret from Hazel.

Richard made the call.

"Hello, Mr. Richard. I've been expecting your call," the voice on the other end said, recognizing him immediately. Richard's reputation in the oil and gas industry preceded him.

Richard gave him details of what he wanted and asked if he was sure he could handle the job.

"I understand the assignment, sir," the investigator assured. "I will deliver in one month's time. The first fifty percent has to be paid to the account I will send to you."

"Not a problem," Richard said. "I'll transfer the first fifteen thousand dollars to your account. Don't forget — we're talking about ten years' details of his life and journey. Don't mess with me and don't leave any stone unturned. Cross your Ts and dot your Is. I'm paying you this much because I love the woman involved, as you know.

"No problem, boss man. We will deliver beyond your expectation." There was a click as the call ended.

Richard got up to sip his coffee, but he knew his mind wouldn't settle, until he saw Hazel. Such was the effect she had on him. He walked out to see his secretary

"Brenda, I need to leave now for an emergency. Please cancel all my meetings. Call the MD of Alpha Oil personally and tell him I'm sorry, but we need to reschedule our appointment."

"Yes, sir," Brenda responded dutifully.

Brenda knew her boss too well to protest, even though the meeting with Alpha Oil was crucial for the company's future. She was aware of what had happened to Richard, although she hadn't been on the guest list—it was very exclusive, with only core family members and friends invited. Richard had only fifty guests on his side, and Hazel had fifty on hers. He had apologized for not being able to include her.

Brenda had heard about the wedding incident and noticed the change in Richard's mood. The contract with Alpha Oil was worth about 4.5 billion dollars, and for Richard to care so little about rescheduling the meeting made her worry. She knew the competition was fierce and decided to call the Managing Director's secretary herself to handle the situation delicately.

"Alpha Oil and Gas, Kikelomo Balch speaking." The secretary's voice was polished with a strong British accent, making Brenda momentarily tongue-tied.

"He-ll-hello, Ms. Balch. This is Brenda Williams from Bay Petroleum. I'm calling to see if we can reschedule the meeting planned for today. My boss has a life-threatening emergency," she said, immediately feeling a pang of guilt for lying.

"A life-threatening emergency? Good Lord, I hope Mr. Akinja is okay. I guess he won't make the meeting today, then?"

"That's correct, ma'am. That's why I'm calling."

"Okay, we'll reschedule. Expect my email."

"Thank you, ma'am. We look forward to the rescheduled meeting. Thanks for your understanding, Ms. Balch."

****

Richard arrived at Hazel's house, and without a word, they embraced in a hug that felt like it could last forever. It was fierce but well-controlled. Hazel wept on Richard's shoulder. She loved him; he brought hope and restoration into her life, adding love to the mix. But she could not shake the thoughts of Ethan from her mind.

Richard gently held her head, his touch filled with affection. For the very first time in all the years of their courtship, Richard let a tear fall. A sudden fear gripped him - how long could he continue fighting for her love? He was not naïve; he knew Ethan would return. His heart sank as he wondered if he was battling the inevitable. He had loved Hazel from the moment they met – this was love in its purest form. Every fiber of his being was devoted to her.

His adrenaline surged, as he suddenly desired Hazel, triggered by the close embrace they had never shared before. He held her more tightly, thinking of how she would have been his by now if not for the wedding disruption. Hazel sensed the change in Richard's breathing and the intensity of his embrace; she knew the signs that he desired her. Gently, she pushed back - they had agreed to wait until marriage. Hazel was a Christian and sex before marriage was a no-no. It was like that even with Ethan, until they were married and he made her a woman.

"Richard…" Hazel began, trying to steady herself. She looked at him and realized that his hands had locked her in an even deeper embrace.

"You need to leave now…" Hazel insisted, not wanting to fall into temptation. "Please don't arouse me. I've been celibate since Ethan d…ied," she stammered. "I'm fine now, but please leave before I become weak with you." She mustered the strength to break the hug.

Richard looked at her fondly. "You know, if Ethan hadn't disrupted our wedding, you would have been mine by now. We would have been one indeed." He stepped back a little, realizing that he had crossed a line.

Hazel understood. "Yes Richard, I would have been yours and nothing would have stopped us tonight. But I need it to be done the right way."

"So, when can we go to the registry? We can't make it big anymore. We need to marry quickly; we can travel to Paris or the UK for our wedding. I want us to marry in two weeks, Hazel."

"Two weeks?" Hazel looked at him, trying to process the rapid pace of everything since the interrupted wedding.

"Yes" Richard said, his gaze intent.

"I…I…" Hazel was at a loss for words.

"Think about it, Hazel. That's the only way you can commit to forever with me. Ethan is a threat to our future, so we might need to stay abroad for a while. I love you, Hazel. We need to set our plans in order - no parents or anyone present. Just you and me. I don't want any more surprises."

Hazel had not expected this to come so quickly. Her mind was torn, still flashing back to memories of Ethan. She could feel Ethan was keeping a close watch on her, unsure of where the feeling came from. She turned to Richard.

"Richard…Give me a little more time to feel better. Two weeks is too soon."

"No, Hazel, two weeks is a long time. I need you, Hazel, I have waited for so long. I love you, so please, get prepared. Your passport is with you, right?"

Hazel nodded, tears dropping from her eyes, as her mind raced.

"No more tears, please," Richard pleaded. He went close to her, held her hand and kissed it.

"I love you, Hazel. I'll be on my way home."

"I love you too, Richard," Hazel said, but her heart was deeply divided. Richard turned and left, trying to keep his emotions in check. He had promised himself not to touch her until they were legally married. Hazel, on the other hand, knew Richard had been a bit too forward tonight, and anything could have happened. She was thankful for the celibacy oath she had made after losing Ethan—not to allow any man until she was married again. It had been ten years since then.

She went to the kitchen and made herself a light tea, deciding to suspend all plans for the Okparas' decorations. She needed to rest. Setting her alarm for 3 a.m. to have her morning prayers, she went to bed.

****

Ethan watched the video for the second time, seething with anger. He was a tech-savvy man and had been watching Hazel very closely. There were secret cameras outside her house, which Ethan's aides monitored; and another in her living room, which Ethan himself monitored. He could not believe what he was seeing – Richard holding his wife. The sight made him want to kill Richard.

The video repulsed Ethan. He had been secretly watching Hazel and Richard, and while he was relieved to hear from their conversation that no one had touched his wife for ten years, he was enraged to see another man hold her so intimately. He understood how Richard felt - Hazel had the same effect on him many years ago.

Ethan made a quick call. "We need to fast-forward Plan 3. I'm not going to watch anyone marry her," he said to the person on the other end. "You don't understand how many years I've longed for my wife and to see her in another's man's arms? Lord, help me!" Ethan paced, his anger boiling over.

"Don't worry, Ethan, we've got this. We'll continue to monitor Richard's moves closely."

"You did well not letting her see the cameras you planted in her house. But I have to move forward with Plan 3 tonight."

"Tonight?" the person on the other end exclaimed, surprise evident in his voice.

"Yes, tonight. I can't let this man take my wife. The way he is going, he is ready to marry her. Plan 3 tonight - take full control of the situation and let me know when to act."

"Yes, boss. I love how you're fighting for your woman."

"I would do this a thousand times for Hazel. She is my wife, and over my dead body will another man have her. And I'm not dying again." He ended the call, aware that he was becoming hysterical. He had endured so many lies, years of captivity, and endless pain and torture—all for loving Hazel. Life had moved on without him for ten years, and he wondered if he could ever reclaim what was lost. He ground his teeth as he had done countless times before.

Ethan turned to the mirror, removing his shirt to reveal the scars on his back and chest - scars he had sustained for Hazel, though unknown to her. He had been declared dead ten years ago and had suffered unspeakably for loving her. It was time for Hazel to learn the truth about the last decade of his life. He examined the large scar on his chest, which had taken the longest to heal. He admired how well-built he had become through hard labor and allowed himself a little smile.

"All this, my love, I went through for you. I'm about to reveal to you the shocking truth of the past ten years. I've always loved you, Hazel—my world. I can't wait to have you back in my arms, where you truly belong, and to make you a woman all over again. Thank you for being faithful to my memory."

Ethan watched the video again, zooming in on Hazel's face and body. His heart swelled with love and pride for her celibacy over the past ten years. He loved Hazel and his passion to pursue her burned brighter. He paced the room a little while and suddenly felt the urge to pray. He knelt down, feeling his pulse rising with anxiety. He trusted God and prayed fervently.

"Father, you have been my hiding place, my secret place, and my covering. You know all the events of my life. You know it was not my fault that I left Hazel. I have been faithful all these years, praying that she would remain untouched. You heard my prayers and delivered me from suffering. Now, as she is about to marry again, I pray earnestly that you fight for the woman you gave me over a decade ago. Keep her for me and rekindle our love. Let my life be a testimony of victory, that you won this battle for me. In Jesus' name, I pray. Amen."

Ethan felt as though voices echoed the "amen" in his bathroom, though he was alone. He had learned to listen to the Holy Spirit. His face was drenched in tears. Only God knew the full story of his survival.

Shortly after, he drove to Hazel's house and, using his phone, monitored her as she stepped into her bedroom to sleep. He planned to stay in the living room till she woke up. It would shock her, he thought, but she would be fine. This had been his plan all along, since Richard was always with her during the day. He accessed the house using the spare keys his men had made for him and sat down quietly. He admired Hazel's taste in internal décor - the cream, green and gold colors were perfect.

Hazel had no idea about Ethan's plans. She did not know he had access to her house nor that he was seated in the living room waiting for her to wake up. Ethan's perfume filled the air, as he stared towards her bedroom. He knew it was best for him to be patient. Just then, his phone beeped silently. The text message threw him off balance: *"Richard is driving into the street; he is coming to Hazel's place, we presume. Leave at once!"*

Plan 3 was not working, and Ethan was furious. He quietly left the house, exiting through the back gate. He was deeply troubled, having barely settled in. Not long after, Richard entered through the front gate, prompting Ethan to ask his men who were on guard and monitoring Hazel, "Didn't he just leave this evening? What is he looking for this night?" He had hired them through an agency, and they seemed to be doing their job well.

"We don't know, boss; but we saw a bunch of flowers in his hands. Now, he's heading to her house," they replied. Ethan monitored Richard through the camera. He was worried to see him in the house again.

Richard placed the flowers in the living room with a note. He then caught a familiar scent—it was the perfume Ethan had worn to disrupt his wedding. Richard was mad. He went to every room in the house and softly opened Hazel's room, finding her sleeping peacefully. He quietly checked her bathroom, closet, and everywhere else. Ethan knew Richard must have caught his scent. He realized Richard had busted him this time as he watched through the live cameras. He was tired of this; he just wanted his wife back.

****

Jackson was renowned for his world-class investigative skills. He was exceptional at uncovering people and events. For a month, he had tried to uncover the truth about Ethan Adebayo but had been unable to find crucial details. He suspected Ethan had conducted some secret operations to erase parts of his profile. Jackson could not trace Ethan's whereabouts for the past ten years, with only the manifest of the plane crash as a clue. He realized that either Ethan was not on the plane or had escaped death at the point of the crash and disappeared for the past decade. His social media accounts were void, and Jackson was getting frustrated trying to uncover his identity.

Jackson noted that Ethan had a gold mining business and had done well for himself, with vast landed properties, making him a very wealthy man. He discovered that Ethan had a sibling, Eniola, and changed his plan to penetrate through her, only to find out that she was married. He was almost giving up when he met an old friend of Helen. Antonia had been very close to Helen, the late twin sister of Hazel. They were best of friends during their youth service. Antonia had been closer to Helen than Hazel, as they shared much in their behavior and life choices.

Jackson decided to approach Antonia, who was into the jewelry business. He made himself a frequent customer, buying top-notch, expensive jewelry from her, pretending it was for his wife. Antonia soon became comfortable with Jackson, expecting more business from him. One day, Jackson offered to take Antonia out for dinner. She was still single and felt privileged to have dinner with him, so she obliged. The single dinner outing soon became more frequent, and Jackson started to subtly inquire about Helen to learn more about Hazel and her husband, Ethan.

During one of their many outings, Jackson carefully steered the conversation towards Helen. That evening, Antonia was a little tipsy and spoke more freely.

"You look so beautiful, Antonia. You remind me of an old lover, Helen," Jackson began, watching Antonia's reaction. She drank some more wine and smiled sadly.

"You know, I used to have a friend by that name," Antonia said, a slight frown creasing her forehead.

"Really? Tell me more about her," Jackson pressed.

Antonia smiled sadly. "She was a masterpiece! But she had some mental health issues, dealing a lot with dissociative disorder, bipolar and depression. She could do something to you and forget it ever happened, and it wouldn't bother her. Sometimes, I thought she was wicked; other times, I wasn't sure where to place her. She was very hardworking and wanted more in life than it offered. She was smart. We got along well during our youth service. She was also a bit crazy, attending a lot of parties—some I went to with her. Honestly, she only dated rich men, powerful politicians. Her connections were solid... but she never found real love." Antonia paused, lost in thought.

"Where's she now?" Jackson asked, more interested now in Helen's story.

"She died in a car accident about nine years ago, one year after her sister's husband died," she concluded.

"So sad..." Jackson feigned innocence and feeling he was not getting enough valuable information for his time. He needed to know more.

"How much do you know about her sister?" he asked

"Not that much but I know they were twins. Now that I think about it..." Antonia began, "Helen fell in love with her sister's husband and told me how she had tried to win him over early on. She was grossly disappointed when he didn't look her way. She told me she would revenge on him for marrying her twin sister...but she never got the chance because Ethan – yes, that was his name - died in a plane crash. And she died not long after."

"Oh, wow! So she liked Ethan, her twin sister's husband? That's strange and doesn't sound good," Jackson said, trying to get more information.

"Helen loved the wrong men. She dated powerful married politicians. At one point she was very powerful herself. She had relationships with the nation's top politicians, who were influential in the military. She used her power a lot."

Jackson's thoughts began to race.

"The plane crash...it must have been devastating," he said.

"I'm not sure anymore. I heard from a close friend that he came back to his wife and didn't die. I don't know what happened, but I wouldn't be surprised if Helen had something to do with it. But whatever she did didn't help her much either."

"Interesting...have some more wine, dear," Jackson suggested, observing that the more Antonia drank, the more she seemed to get lost in memories of her friend.

"So, where could Ethan have been since he was declared dead?" Jackson asked, more interested in piecing the puzzle together.

"Not sure..." She shrugged. "I would have known better if Helen were alive, because she kept a close watch on him."

"Hmmm...close watch," Jackson repeated, unsure how to proceed since Helen was dead.

"Jackson...I'm so sorry to bore you with stories that you have no idea about," Antonia said, seeming to come back to her senses.

"Oh no, Antonia, it's interesting to hear these stories sometimes. I just wonder how the guy you talked about – Ethan - was on the manifest of the plane crash but didn't board the plane. Makes me wonder if someone was playing some games," he said with a wry smile.

"Strange..." Antonia offered. "Especially since he came back to his wife."

"And that's Helen's sister. What's her name?"

"Hazel, Hazel Adebayo."

"They must be happy together now, huh?" He added, trying to gauge her reaction.

"Well, I heard from the grapevine she was getting married to another great guy, but Ethan showed up - an old friend of Helen and Hazel told me."

"Oh wow....so what is she going to do now?" Jackson probed further.

"I really don't know. She will make up her mind on that, who disappears for ten years and then comes back to claim his wife who had moved on?" she asked casually.

"So you don't think she will go back to Ethan?" Jackson hoped.

"Well, she loved him, but I haven't seen her in ages, and we weren't even close at the time I knew Helen. She's a very calm person and meek too. I guess she'll pray to know what to do. I heard the other guy is rich too. *Meennnn*, she is so lucky with the moneybags!" Antonia concluded.

"Hmmmnn" Jackson muttered casually, glad to have this piece of information recorded. The whereabouts of Ethan at the time of the crash remained a mystery he had to unravel. Richard was already getting impatient to know who Ethan was and Jackson was trying so hard to get tangible information for him. It seemed like the ten years of Ethan's disappearance had no records or history; he must have done well to hide this information, Jackson thought.

CHAPTER EIGHT

Everyone has a wilderness experience
Born of a woman you must pass through yours
Pray the evil days pass quickly
So indeed, you can chant, "Victory has come!"

Ethan sat in bed and allowed his mind to drift back to the sequence of events in his life that had led to this moment. Two hundred hefty military men had surrounded the mall where he was shopping. He needed to buy some items before heading to the airport to catch his flight. He was oblivious to the military presence until they, along with some police officers, accosted him.

"Are you Ethan Adebayo?" one of the officers asked, flashing his badge.

Ethan looked puzzled, realizing the entire troop had come for him. He hesitated and looked at his phone, intending to call his lawyers.

"How can I help you, sirs?" Ethan asked respectfully.

"You are needed at the police station right away for questioning. You have the right to remain silent. Anything you say can and will be used against you in a court of law..."

"May I know what this is all about, please? I need to contact my lawyers and my wife first."

"Yes, Mr. Adebayo. You can do that at the station. We need to move now." Ethan knew better than to argue, as the scene was intimidating, and he resolved to use his lawyers later. What he did not know was that this would be his last time out and about for the next ten years. He was escorted into one of the waiting vehicles; he counted almost ten in the parking lot, all there just to pick him up. He was slightly agitated as his phone was seized; he was unsure of what was going on as he could not reach anyone.

As soon as Ethan got to the station, his journey into ten years of incarceration began. He could not reach the outside world or demand justice. At this time, the military regime was in power, the country was going through chaos, and many legal institutions were on strike, preventing him from even seeing a judge. He could not get justice, however he tried.

After a week of being locked up, he was told he had a visitor. When he came to see who it was, he was surprised to see Helen.

"What are you doing here, Helen? How did you know where I am? How is Hazel?" he asked, noticing she was in the company of soldiers.

"Aww," she said mockingly. "You thought you were so big, right? You thought you could have the best life with stupid Hazel? What does she have that I haven't offered you? But you chose her over me. I did all to win your love, but you kept shoving me aside like I was nothing."

"What is all this, Helen? Did you do this to me?" Ethan asked, his eyes wide open.

"Oh, shut up, Ethan. The world is no longer yours— gold, land, properties, and love. You are a dead man to the world."

'No, I am not dead, I will come out alive."

"Over my dead body, Ethan. You will rot in here!"

Ethan had never seen this side of Helen before. She looked cold-blooded and deranged; her stare was chilling.

"You were announced as dead in the plane crash that happened a week ago—so timely for what I needed it to look like. While I was thinking, I heard about the plane crash that evening, and all I needed to do was make your disappearance look like a plane crash... " She laughed wickedly, stepped a little forward, and blew Ethan a mocking kiss. Her face contorted in anger again, as she said, "Your name is on the manifest; Hazel is mourning her dear loss, and I can't be happier that we've leveled up. You hurt me, Ethan. I fell in love with you and tried to let you know multiple times, but you were so disrespectful and dismissive. This is what your arrogance has cost you."

"Are you in your right mind, Helen? You mean you planned all this because I refused to sleep with you? I am married to your own twin sister. Who does that?"

"Quiet!" she roared, looking wild. The officer monitoring the visit quickly glanced at her, wondering why her voice had suddenly become menacing. "You thought you had it all. I consulted with the high and mighty and pulled a few strings on the manifest...." She smiled sweetly now, her mood changing as if she were acting in a play. "And now that you're here...you won't live to tell this story. Hell has no fury as a woman scorned!"

Dumfounded, Ethan stared at Helen, as his world finally crumbled. He didn't know he had been declared dead. "Oh Lord," he muttered. "Hazel! My dear Hazel..." He whimpered as reality hit him hard. "I am alive, an enemy did this to us." He wept bitterly, not because he was declared dead, but because he knew how traumatic this would be for Hazel. After a minute, he stood up defiantly and called the officer to take him back to his cell.

Ethan was denied justice, access, and hearing. He had no lawyer, no advocate, and no one to help him in prison. He was housed with condemned criminals, and Helen often visited to taunt him and make his life harder. He prayed for years, but the answer seemed far from coming. Twice, he was stabbed in prison sustaining injury when fights broke out among the inmates. He stayed out of trouble and kept praying for an exit, not knowing how to find one.

****

Today marked the fifth year of Ethan's incarceration. He was in the queue for his terrible breakfast of watery pap and the local bean cake. He was not feeling well this morning and had barely managed to rise from his wooden bed, his body aching and sore. As he shuffled along the line, he listened to the news echoing through the big hallway leading to the dining area. There was talk of a recent protest that had resulted in some arrests, but thankfully, those people had been released. His heart grew heavy with sorrow as he lamented the state of the country's justice system.

One of the inmates, Danjuma—though everyone called him Dan—was behind him, nudging him to move faster. Dan, like Ethan, was a victim of cruelty and injustice. But while Ethan had never been tried, Dan had been sentenced to life imprisonment for a crime he did not commit. He had been charged with the first-degree murder of his stepmother. Dan had confessed to Ethan that he was innocent, explaining that he had discovered that his stepmother was cheating on his father and had confided in a neighbor. Unknown to him, the neighbor was also involved with his stepmother and, driven by jealousy, had orchestrated her murder, making it look like Dan was the culprit.

As Ethan moved forward with a heavy heart, he pitied those who, like him, had been denied a fair hearing. Some of them were wealthy but their money could not match the power of their enemies. He had tried countless times to contact his lawyers and the outside world but to no avail. He even repeatedly pleaded with Helen but she was bent on keeping him locked up. Resigned to his fate, he often wondered how his business was faring. He thought of his dear Hazel, Eniola, his sister, and his parents. It seemed only a miracle could save him now.

He collected his meal and retreated to his corner to eat. Just as he was about to bless his food, a song welled up in his spirit. He began to hum the tune softly under his breath; then, feeling a renewed strength in his spirit and body, he started to sing:

I've found a friend in Jesus, he's everything to me,
He's the fairest of ten thousand to my soul;
The lily of the valley, in him alone I see
All I need to cleanse and make me fully whole.
In sorrow he's my comfort, in trouble he's my stay,
He tells me every care on him to roll.

Refrain:
He's the lily of the valley, the bright and morning star,
He's the fairest of ten thousand to my soul.

He all my griefs has taken, and all my sorrows borne,
In temptation he's my strong and mighty tower;
I've all for him forsaken, I've all my idols torn

From my heart, and now he keeps me by his power.

Though all the world forsake me, and Satan tempt me sore,

Through Jesus I shall safely reach the goal.

He'll never, never leave me, nor yet forsake me here,

While I live by faith and do his blessed will;

A wall of fire about me, I've nothing now to fear,

With his manna he my hungry soul shall fill.

Then sweeping up to Glory, I'll see his blessed face

Where rivers of delight shall ever flow.

Soon, other prisoners who knew the song sang along. Even the staff found themselves singing. A revival took place, and many were moved to tears. Some came to Ethan, asking him to pray for them. Startled, he offered only a simple prayer of repentance and hope. He knelt down, and so did everyone else. They joined hands and prayed, and that day marked a significant turning point in the lives of many prisoners. It was a time of healing, even though there seemed to be no hope or help on the horizon. The strength they found in the song and the ensuing fellowship made that day a blessed one.

Ethan prayed again, hopeful that he would soon be released and allowed to go home. The next morning, he began a seven-day fast, clinging to the hope that a miracle was still possible.

****

Ten long years after Ethan's incarceration, he was finally freed from prison, along with several others. The long-serving military head of state had decided to hand over to the recently elected civilian president. One of the immediate reforms the new government embarked upon was releasing those who had been imprisoned without trial for years and had good standing.

Upon his release, Ethan reunited with his family, who were shocked to see him alive. He recounted everything that had happened and revealed how Helen had been behind his ordeal, as she had confessed to him in prison. His family's joy knew no bounds; his parents, in particular, were glad that their prayers had been answered. Their lives had not been the same since his departure, and they were relieved that he had not died in the reported plane crash.

Despite his freedom, Ethan felt a deep sense of injustice for the years of abuse and deprivation of his legal rights. His sister updated him on what had transpired in Hazel's life. Through his time in prison, Ethan had learned never to divulge his plans to anyone. Prison had taught him wisdom, stamina, and strategy. Though he planned to sue the Federal Government of Nigeria for imprisoning him for ten years without trial, he decided that could wait until he got Hazel back.

His wealth had remained intact, thanks to his remarkable family, especially his sister, Eniola. She had also kept a close watch on Hazel and discovered that she was getting married in two days. Determined to stop the wedding, Ethan had vowed to do whatever it took. This was why he had shown up at Hazel's wedding with the hired military troop he got through a top rated security agency.

CHAPTER NINE

Love is like the shades of the rainbow;
Some colors are bright, and some look dim
But, in the end, it delivers its promises;
Never to destroy is what God said
Love is pure and not destructive.

Ethan retrieved from the safe the document that had been delivered to him a few days ago. Despite his religious leaning, he could not help feeling relieved that Helen was gone. She had wanted to be cremated, so she was burnt to ashes. He had not actually prayed for her death, but he was sure it was her evils that caught up with her.

Ethan was a little perplexed and unsure how to tell Hazel what truly happened to her sister. He could not tell everything all at once; she might faint. He locked the paperwork back in the safe and gently rose. He still had the task of winning back her love from the arms of Richard.

****

Hazel was fully recovered and ready to take on the day. She had rested well the previous night, oblivious to the fact that Ethan was monitoring her. She wondered why Richard had asked her to come to his office that morning and to hurry. It worried her; she knew it had to be important and urgent. She had her bath and got dressed in simple jeans and a sweatshirt; the weather was cool, as it had rained early that morning.

As soon as she entered the living room, she saw the flowers and the small gift bag that Richard had brought. She smiled when she saw the note. She was glad Richard had been over to visit since he was the only one with access to her house. She loved the smell of his cologne, but she felt a little strange about this scent. Still, she did not think too much of it.

Ethan, on the other hand, was furious and grossly disappointed that Richard had detected his presence, and he vowed to do everything to block Hazel from him. He knew he needed to act quickly and kept checking the camera in Hazel's house. He was lucky to see her making a call to Richard. He listened to her side of the conversation and knew that Richard wanted her to meet him somewhere, promising to text her the location. Ethan resolved to use other tactics to get an audience with Hazel without scaring her. He decided to confront her as soon as she left the house. He was not going to waste time; he needed to act swiftly.

Hazel stepped out and made her way to her car, driving through the streets of Lagos. Ethan had his men take their positions. They were to hit her car and delay her, allowing him to make an appearance. He was becoming desperate to see her and did not trust going back into her house, knowing Richard already suspected him. He called his ally.

"Brian, are you ready?"

"Yes, boss. It's going to be a subtle impact from the back. She is taking the Allen Avenue T-junction, and we plan to follow and hit around Adeniyi Jones."

"Excellent. I'm right on her trail."

Hazel, unaware of what was going on, was driving. She was as fresh as the morning rose and as beautiful as ever. She wondered why Richard had asked her to take this route, and it made her even more worried. She knew Richard loved her, but she briefly thought of Ethan, and a cold shiver ran down her spine. She knew she felt something for Ethan; Ethan had been everything to her at some point. He had loved her beyond words and made her feel like a queen. She wondered if the man she saw at the altar was really Ethan or if someone was playing a cruel trick on her. She was confused.

Suddenly, she felt the impact from behind and had to stop. She was angry but tried to stay calm. Who had the nerve to hit her car that way? She thought as she remained frozen for a second. Just then, another car veered and hit her from the front, suggesting a multiple-car accident, with her as the sole victim. She realized she could not move forward or backward. She stepped out, furious, but tried to calm herself down. The two drivers were men who looked like they were in a hurry and on their way to work. They were apologetic and expressed their remorse. She examined the damage; it was not too severe in the back or front. In any case, she was not in the mood to argue and really wanted to go see Richard.

"I'm so sorry," the driver from behind said. "I was in a hurry. My wife is in labor and I have to go pick her up to the hospital."

"Please, be careful next time. You've caused some damage to my car," she responded. She knew it would not be a problem to fix the car. She would take it to the dealership, and her insurance deductible should cover the damage. Her car was an expensive Mercedes-Benz 300 SLR Uhlenhaut Coupe, which cost an average of $145,000,000. It was about the most expensive car in the world. Richard had given it to her as a birthday gift last year. She had protested that it was too expensive, but he insisted that it was the least of the cars his future wife would drive.

"It's okay, sir," she said respectfully to the man who was speaking with her. She noticed that the other driver, the one who had veered into her lane, was approaching, and she knew he had some excuses too. She was upset about it all, but tried to calm down.

"I'm so sorry, ma'am. I have an interview this morning and was a bit distracted, causing the collision," the second driver said.

Hazel turned to face him, speechless. Her morning was not going well. She knew she could not hold these men responsible, as her car was very expensive, and she doubted they could afford to fix it. Most drivers did not even carry insurance, she thought. She waved her hand.

"You should be more careful. I have an urgent meeting to attend," she said, turning to make her way back to her car. She opened the door to sit and was shocked to see someone entering from the passenger side. It was Ethan, and he sprang into action immediately.

"Get in the car now, Hazel. I need to speak with you," he demanded. Hazel was thunderstruck. She got in but could not drive. Ethan asked her to move to the passenger seat, as he got out to take over the driver seat. He winked at his two allies outside, stepped back in and started the car.

"Ethan, is it really you?" Hazel asked calmly, staring hard at his sideburns. She recalled how she always teased him about having a perfect side profile.

"Yes, Hazel, it is me. Ethan." He moved the car out of the terrible traffic and drove straight to a gas station to park.

"My Hazel, it has been so difficult seeing you, but I have been so close by...I watched you at the hospital, at home and everywhere. I knew I needed to see you."

He faced Hazel now that he had parked.

"Hazel, I didn't die. It was a huge lie, a deception from the pit of hell. I need to explain everything to you, but I need your time and attention."

Hazel was overwhelmed with emotions. She did not know whether to be happy or sad for seeing Ethan. She realized, looking at him, that she still had feelings for him. She briefly recalled how those arms used to hold her. She realized he still wanted her back. Hazel looked at him and didn't know what to say.

"...and I found you," Ethan finished, but Hazel hadn't heard a word. She was lost in her thoughts.

"Pardon?"

"Hazel, I know you're confused by everything that's happening now, but you are my wife, and you belong to me. It's been ten years, and I promise you I've never been with another woman. Hazel, what happened was a setup. I was imprisoned for ten years and pronounced dead."

Hazel looked shocked and opened her mouth.

"What?" She looked even more confused. "But I recall seeing your name on the passenger list. You were on a plane from Abuja, your plane crashed."

"That's utter nonsense, Hazel! I was left to rot in jail for all those years. It wasn't a conventional jail, Hazel. I have so much to tell you."

"Who did this to you, Ethan? It's been ten years! I was faithful to your memory. I was even admitted to a psychiatric hospital for a year after I heard you died in that crash."

Hazel was a whirlwind of emotions. Ethan wanted to hug her but restrained himself.

"I'm so sorry, Hazel. The enemy wanted us apart and seemed to have momentarily succeeded. But I'm back now."

He looked at her intently. "Will you come back to me, Hazel, so we can build what we started over a decade ago? My feelings for you haven't changed."

"Come back to you, Ethan? Oh Lord, I'm engaged to Richard! He was the one who stood by me and helped me to overcome the pain. I met him three years ago, years after your supposed death. He was my first and only relationship after you. I couldn't love anyone else; I couldn't enter another relationship. I lost you and Helen around the same time. It was so hard for me, Ethan. When I saw you at the wedding, I thought I was seeing a ghost. The wedding was disrupted, and I haven't been the same since, but I made my commitment to Richard, Ethan."

Tears streamed down Hazel's face.

Poor Hazel, Ethan thought.

"Richard wants to marry you, but I can't just stand by and watch any other man take you. If this had happened sooner, I wouldn't have been able to forgive myself, and I wouldn't have been able to fight for you. I believe God made my escape to be this time so I can claim my love back. Yes, Richard may be a great guy, but you don't belong to him, Hazel."

Hazel became totally overwhelmed. She was happy Ethan had not died in the crash, but she needed proof she was not being deceived. She was suddenly on her guard.

"Prove to me it's really you, Ethan," She said calmly.

Ethan stared at her. His Hazel looking more radiant and more beautiful than ever. The feelings inside him surged, an overwhelming desire to hold her again. Without thinking, he reached for her face and without warning, kissed her. Hazel was speechless. The spark was electrifying, and she lost all her defenses, kissing him back passionately. She held his face and looked into his eyes.

"I didn't mean to kiss you…but is this really you, my Ethan?"

Hazel vividly remembered the emotions and butterflies she always felt when they were intimate years ago. But then she remembered Richard and pulled away almost instantly, suddenly feeling guilty.

Ethan looked into her eyes. "It's him, isn't it? You remembered Richard and felt like you were cheating?"

Hazel covered her face with her hands, more confused and upset that she had let Ethan touch and kiss her so quickly. Even though he was her husband, it did not feel right. She had committed to marrying Richard, the man who had kept her going and given her a reason to live again. Just then, her phone rang, and she guessed who it was.

"He is waiting for me, Ethan."

"I know…He's so insecure that he is probably going to ask you to leave your apartment right away." Ethan laughed sarcastically.

"Why would he say so?"

"You'll see. He thinks I might know where you live and have access to you," Ethan said, knowing what had happened the previous night, which was not known to Hazel.

"I don't think he is insecure; he is just very protective of me. He once slapped a cousin of his because he was flirting with me. He will go to that length for me," she replied.

101

"Ethan, a lot has happened…a lot has truly happened. Time healed my wounds from your sudden departure. I have always loved you, been always faithful to you. From the last time you touched me, the morning you left to board that plane, until now, no one – and I mean no one – has been with me. I've kept myself, and I gradually fell in love with Richard. I've always loved you, but now it's more complicated."

"I know how you feel, Hazel, and you know I don't give up. I've fought for you for so long, and Richard can't stop me. I should have access to you, Hazel. I should be able to make you mine again. You're my wife. I never died, and you will always be Mrs. Ethan Adebayo. Let that sink in," Ethan said.

The events of the day were overpowering for Hazel. She had seen Ethan again after the wedding episode. He was back to claim her, and Richard was not going to back down. She recounted everything she had heard from both men, each professing genuine love for her, and she felt torn between the two. Hazel wondered what her life was turning into. At thirty-four, she did not have much time. She wanted a family and her own children, but she needed to choose carefully between the two men.

****

Richard was happy to see Hazel when she arrived. He gave her a slight hug and ushered her into his private waiting room. She sat down and took a sip of the pineapple juice prepared for her - her favorite, and something Richard always made sure to have for her. She kept staring at Richard, unsure how to proceed after the encounter with Ethan.

Richard sat with her. "Believe it or not but Ethan got into your apartment yesterday. Your apartment is bugged, and he knows what you do and who you talk to." Richard said convincingly. He was not a novice in this game, he thought.

"What?" Hazel felt vulnerable knowing that her home was electronically monitored.

"How did you know this?"

"I could smell him, Hazel. I had been over to drop your flowers there and as soon as I came in, I smelled his strong perfume, the exact one he had on when he disrupted our wedding."

"Oh Lord, Richard, that's not proof. I did notice something different in my house, but no, I don't believe he has access."

"He does and I need to get you checked into a hotel until I can find a better place for you. Please trust me."

"Stop, Richard. Stop being paranoid; it's not that serious."

"You were with him weren't you?" Richard asked, looking her straight in the eye. Hazel held her breath for a second and nodded.

"Someone had hit my car from behind and another from the front. Both drivers came to apologize, and then Ethan showed up. I was beyond shocked; he drove me somewhere, and we talked."

"There was no accident, Hazel. It was all planned. I know Ethan and all he is doing to catch your attention."

"Oh wow! Well, he must have done a good job because I never suspected him. But how do you know these things, Richard? Have you been spying on him?»

"No, Hazel," Richard replied, not wanting to reveal too much. Thanks to Jackson; he and his team have been able to track some things that Ethan has been doing.

"I just know his type." Richard offered.

He turned to Hazel and embraced her. "We need to travel abroad and get married as soon as possible. Otherwise, Ethan will do everything to get you back. I've been the love of your life for the last three years. I want you to be my wife, Hazel. I can't wait any longer. So, first, I need to get you out of that apartment. It is bugged. Ethan knows everything going on there. I'm certain of it. His perfume was heavy in your house. Please trust me."

Hazel felt butterflies in her stomach. She loved Richard and who he was. His love was sincere and consistent. He had shunned everyone who questioned his relationship with a widow and had stood by her side. He was incredibly handsome, and she did not want to break his heart. But she was also concerned about Ethan. Ethan was every woman's dream, but she had grown to love Richard deeply and to rely on him. However, after that brief kiss with Ethan in her car, she knew Ethan had recaptured her heart. She loved Ethan too.

"Is that why you asked me to come to your office? So he wouldn't hear us? Please, Richard. We're too grown for this," she said dismissively. She did not believe Ethan would bug her house and was not going to leave. Richard decided to drop the subject for now.

CHAPTER TEN

Life is seed and harvest
Life gives you back what you feed it
Sow well and you will reap well too.

Mrs. Bukola Akinja was a retired oil mogul, with significant influence and affluence. Trained in Britain, she had an impeccable British accent. As expected of a woman of her status, she had many concerns and preoccupations. Of late, however, her primary concern had been the love life of her son, Richard. From the time he told her about Hazel till the time of their botched wedding, she had gently expressed her misgivings but was careful enough not to interfere with his decision. When Richard informed her of the latest development involving Ethan, she was quick to remind him of her stance.

"Richie," Mrs. Akinja began. "I want you to have a good life, my son. I had my reservations about your choice of Hazel. I want you to be happy again, Richie. Hazel is very complicated. Her husband never died, apparently. What sort of joke was that, Richie?"

"Oh Lord, Mom, please. If you can't comfort me, don't add to my pain. You never liked Hazel."

"No, I just had the Holy Spirit warn me about her and you never listened. She is not your wife, Richard. May God open your eyes, my love. I called to check on you. I love you, son. I'll be in Abuja next week. I'll visit you and stay over a couple of days."

"Yes, Mom, please come visit. And with all due respect, Hazel deserves a good life. She didn't know her husband was alive. There's a lot I'm learning too. We'll talk when you're around."

Richard said his goodbyes and got thinking. He knew his mother had always been right about things, from his childhood surgery to his choice of college and career. She had met Hazel, heard her story, and warned Richard not to get involved with her. She liked Hazel as a person but felt she wasn't the right choice for her son. With the failed wedding ceremony, Richard realized his mother had been right once again.

Despite Hazel's declarations of love, Richard felt a sudden gap in their relationship. He wondered how long her love would last and decided to speed up the wedding before it was too late.

****

Helen had struggled with mental health issues for a long time. She had very low self-esteem and had seen a psychiatrist who had prescribed medication for her bipolar disorder, a chronic mental health condition that causes dramatic changes in mood, energy levels and behavior. Her parents had noticed her mood swings but did not understand it was a mental disorder. Helen did not know why she had extreme mood swings until she left for college and was advised by a friend to see a psychiatrist. She was prescribed lithium and had to monitor her blood levels regularly, but she found it burdensome and noticed that it gave her suicidal thoughts. Often, she was not compliant with her medication.

Helen's twin sister did not exhibit any signs of mental disorder, and Helen could not understand why she was different. Despite her struggles, Helen's mental health remained a significant issue. After orchestrating Ethan's imprisonment, she decided to distance herself from her family and align herself with Ethan if he ever changed his mind.

Barely a year after Ethan's supposed plane crash, Helen staged an accident and made her family believe she had died. She relocated to Port Harcourt, changed her identity and started a new life. She stopped seeing her therapist and psychiatrist, abandoning her therapy and medication.

Helen struggled with her emotions, sometimes feeling sad about her lack of success, compared to her twin sister, and at other times happy to be getting money from wealthy married men. She had no attachment to her family, which made her transition smooth. She knew she could not have Ethan, despite trying for years. She did not use her connections to get him out of prison and resigned herself to the life she had chosen. However, when she learned that Ethan was among those set free due to the lack of a fair trial, she knew she was in trouble.

****

Hazel woke up with a pounding headache. She felt a void inside, and a wave of sadness washed over her, as she remembered Helen. A brief smile crept across her face at the memory. She loved her sister deeply and had not missed her this much until now. Reaching for her phone, she pulled up an old photo she had saved.

"May your soul rest in peace, Helen. I wish you were here today. We were born the same day and the same hour. Yes, I came before you by a few minutes. I wish you had a child or someone who could remind me of you other than your memories. I wish you hadn't embarked on that journey that led to your tragic accident and claimed your life." She kissed the picture and got up.

Just then, her phone rang. The number was unfamiliar, but due to the nature of her business, she always answered calls, as clients could come from anywhere.

"Hello," Hazel answered.

"Hazel Victoria Adebayo, the wife of my youth. Blessed and full of grace. How are you today?"

110

Hazel recognized the salutation immediately. For many months during their marriage, Ethan had greeted her this way in the morning, showering her with prayers and speaking great things into her life. Hazel hesitated for a second.

"Hazel, how are you doing? I know you can hear me."

"Et... Eth... Ethan..." she stuttered.

"Hazel, how are you? This is the third time I'm asking."

"I am fine, Ethan."

"Hold on for someone, Hazel," Ethan said into the phone.

"Hello," a familiar voice echoed from the other side. It was Hazel's college friend, Eniola, who was also Ethan's sister.

"Eniola..."

"Yes, dear Hazel, it's so good to speak with you again. I'm with Ethan here; we're in a meeting, and I thought I'd say hello."

Hazel remembered Eniola and was happy to hear from her. Eniola had stood with her during those trying moments when she thought she had lost Ethan. She had stayed with Hazel for about a month before travelling back to London, where she was based.

"Enny!" Hazel called again, smiling at the sweet memories. She recalled how Eniola would constantly check on her after she returned to London. Eniola, like Ethan, was business-oriented and often travelled between London and Lagos at the time. She was a true friend. Hearing her voice brought back more memories for Hazel.

They chatted endlessly on the phone, excited to reconnect. Hazel almost forgot her sadness and her appointments for the day while talking to Eniola—it was refreshing.

"It's been a while. I'd love to see you…" Eniola cooed.

Hazel knew this was a ploy from Ethan, but she could not refuse to see Eniola, who was one of the kindest souls she had ever met.

"Sure, Eniola. You know, this morning I was thinking of Helen…" Hazel began. She knew Eniola was aware of Helen, even though they weren't close friends. "I miss her."

Eniola spoke quickly, aware of something Hazel did not know.

"I understand, Hazel. May her soul continue to rest," she replied, then added, "Can we have dinner this evening or tomorrow? I'm flying back to London over the weekend and would really like to see you."

"Tomorrow will be better, Enny. I look forward to seeing you too."

They hung up and Hazel knew immediately that Eniola's call was orchestrated by Ethan, who wanted to see her. She knew Ethan would be present. She tried to be fair to Richard, but each time she tried, she found justifications for why she still needed to be with Ethan. This was becoming increasingly complicated for her mind and spirit. She had thought she could manage it and be with Richard, but she found herself softening towards Ethan again. She remembered how Ethan had supported her, sponsored her and established her decoration and event planning business. He had not let her work but had encouraged her to have her own business.

Her phone rang again. It was Richard. Richard Akinja was deeply in love with Hazel. She answered with a little smile; she still loved Richard and cared about him.

"Hello, Richard."

"Hi, my love, you sound cheerful!" Richard noted.

"Oh yes, an old friend reconnected with me. I just finished speaking with her," Hazel said truthfully.

Richard wondered who it was but did not want to press any further.

"Happy Birthday in advance," Richard said. Hazel then realized that her birthday was the next day – May 13th. She was turning 35! She smiled, wondering how she had forgotten the month and date. Hazel appreciated Richard's thoughtfulness.

"Thank you, Richard."

"I have a surprise for you tomorrow. What is your schedule like in the evening?"

Hazel felt awkward, realizing she had committed to Eniola. Then she realized that Ethan must have known and only used Eniola as a front for her birthday, even though Eniola had not mentioned it. Hazel had not realized how close her birthday was. Her mind had been so preoccupied, and she realized that the sadness she felt earlier was due to her thoughts of her twin sister.

"Hazel? Are you there?"

"Yes, sorry. I got distracted. I just thought of Helen the moment you wished me a happy birthday."

"Oh, I'm sorry, Hazel. I didn't mean to remind you of Helen. May her soul rest in peace."

"Amen. Thanks, Richard."

"You're welcome, my love. But I'm still waiting for your answer. I'd like to take you out for dinner tomorrow evening." Richard knew he had to bring her mind back to the present matter.

Hazel was in a big fix. She had already agreed to meet Eniola, and now Richard wanted to spend the same time with her. She was trying to figure out what to say.

"Hazel, do you have plans for tomorrow evening?"

"Yes, Richard, my friend Eniola has already booked tomorrow evening with me. It's been a while since I have seen her...she's lives in London but now in town," Hazel added.

"Okay, I will bring your gift to the house earlier. I love you, my dear."

Hazel was not sure how to respond. She loved him, and she loved Ethan too. But she realized that her love for each was becoming different. Her love for Richard was ever there, but her feelings for Ethan were rekindling. She did not know how to respond but, knowing Richard, she had to reply in the affirmative.

"I love you too, Richard."

"Thank you for saying that, Hazel."

"I've always loved you, Richard. Ethan was...is...my husband. I don't know if it's right to say these words to you, Richard. My mind is in two places. But I meant what I said; I still love you, Richard."

"Let's get married immediately, Hazel. I hate to pressure you, but when will you be ready? I can book a flight this weekend for a private wedding," Richard offered.

"I can't do that now, Richard. Please allow me time to sort out my emotions and life. Ethan is back, and that changes everything."

"Ethan died ten years ago. I don't understand this. Honey, you know I won't let go. I'll bring your gift tomorrow morning. I'll call you later today."

Hazel walked to the bathroom on wobbly legs. She realized she needed to make a definite decision about her relationships. She needed counsel, she needed help, and she wanted to be sure she was treading the right path. She remembered the love she shared with Ethan. If what he said was real, it was not his fault for going through incarceration and being locked away. She did not understand why, but she knew Ethan genuinely loved her and cared for her. She knew Richard cared deeply too. She got up and thought of a new plan; she had to prove their love all over again. She needed the guidance of the Holy Spirit.

****

Hazel heard the doorbell ring, it was early, she thought, just barely making it out of the bedroom, she peeped to see who it was and noted a delivery man in uniform, he looked like he had a parcel to deliver to her, Hazel opened the door and was greeted by the man

"Good morning ma'am, I am looking for Hazel Adebayo" The man said with a huge smile.

Taken aback and wondering what this was, Hazel responded.

"How can I help you?"

"Oh hi ma'am, I have a parcel to deliver to you, you are to sign on this part of the paper and this box is yours. Happy birthday!" The man said officiously.

"Thank you!" Hazel smiled, knowing this gift was most definitely from Richard. She signed and collected the box and documents, she went inside and opened the box, she saw a key and a note.

"Happy birthday my forever lilies,
I love you always
-Richard Akinja

She immediately called Richard beaming with smiles but a silently troubled heart.

"Thank you Richard, you always spoil me...What key is this?

"A smart house in Banana Island, it's a duplex and well furnished, it a vacation home. I love you so much."

Hazel smiled in appreciation, unsure if she was going to collect this house now that she was more at a crossroads. She knew not to reject it at this time, they chatted for a while and hung up.

****

Eniola brought a small box of chocolates and an expensive perfume for Hazel's birthday. She had searched for the restaurant on the internet, doing this on behalf of her brother. Eniola was one of the happiest people on earth seeing her brother return to the family; she was grateful for his life. Like Hazel, she had mourned her brother daily—his supposed death had caused her a lot of emotional turbulence, especially as they were close siblings.

Hazel arrived at the restaurant, which was bustling with activity. Eniola had contacted the manager to reserve a wing of the restaurant for the entire evening. It cost a good amount of money, but Ethan was paying. The table was set for dinner, and Eniola waited for Hazel. When Hazel showed up, Eniola noticed she looked even more beautiful than she had been ten years ago. She was not as slim as before, there was a little more flesh to her, but she still maintained a good shape and muscle tone. Eniola stood up and went to hug her. They exchanged pleasantries, sat down, and ordered their food. Eniola observed Hazel and made up her mind that Hazel was still, and would always be, the perfect match for Ethan.

The waiter brought a box that was meant to be another birthday gift. Hazel was pleasantly surprised as she had already received a box of chocolate and perfume from Eniola.

"Why are you going through so much trouble?" Hazel said with a smile. She opened the box and saw a car key. She looked at Eniola in surprise.

"It's the key to the latest Ferrari F8 Spider, costing my darling brother a whopping $302,500 coming in your favorite color – green – and custom-made just for you, Hazel. Well-branded for you. With love from the man behind you."

Hazel immediately looked back and, there stood Ethan, looking stunning and breathtaking. She opened her mouth and closed it again. He looked more striking and well-groomed than she remembered. She recalled their early married life, how he loved to look extra good and make a great impression with his outfits. She smelled his cologne, and right then, she knew she still loved Ethan. It was different, it was refreshing - this man had suffered on her behalf. Although she still had not yet pieced everything together, she knew he was incarcerated because of her and he had come out and searched for her again.

Ethan took steady steps towards her, looking at the love of his life - the one he bore many scars for. He was maimed on his toes because of her. His love was pure and perfect; she was his joy and gladness. Hazel! Her name was refreshing, and she looked the most beautiful woman on earth. As he approached, he observed how well she looked, considering every detail—her shape, her tone, her skin, and her glow. He looked into her eyes, and the music in the atmosphere changed. This was a deliberate move to set the mood for Hazel.

Eniola watched them with so much joy. She understood that Hazel had moved on just three years ago when she met Richard, but she could not blame her. Hazel had been true to the memory of Ethan before starting to date again and did not rush into marriage. She had waited ten years and kept herself. Eniola admired Hazel; she was a beauty to behold. She remembered how men fought for her attention in college and how lucky her brother was to get her attention, even when Helen was after him and threw herself at him.

"To the most beautiful woman I have ever met, the one I suffered for and bear scars and bruises for, the only reason I fight and beam with gladness—Hazel Adebayo. Thank you for not changing my name, thank you for being loyal for seven years before dating Richard. Thank you for not letting anyone touch you these past ten years. I love you and I am back to continue my life with you. I am sorry for Richard, but you will always be mine. Happy Birthday, beautiful. I love you now and will never leave you again."

He held her close to him and asked for her hand to dance. Hazel was still in a bit of shock at all that had happened - her birthday gift, Eniola coming to dinner, and seeing Ethan, which she had kind of anticipated but did not expect to happen this way.

"Excuse me, may I have this dance?" Ethan held her by the waist, and an electric current ran through Hazel's veins. Ethan's hands always did that magic to her. She loved her gift of Ferrari F8 Spider. She was still in awe and overwhelming shock.

She finally found her voice. "Thank you, Ethan, but you did not have to spend so much on a car. My car is working just fine."

Ethan smiled, recalling how prudent his wife was. "I'll do much more, Hazel. Love is deeper than the ocean and thicker than blood."

The night went by quickly. The dinner started 7 p.m. and took up the whole evening. Ethan took Hazel back home and had his driver bring Hazel's car back with him. Hazel was tired and sleepy and Ethan helped her into the house. He kissed her forehead, his hands encircling her body

"Please, Ethan, don't touch me," Hazel pleaded, remembering Richard. She felt conflicted.

"I should because you are my wife and I have every right to, but I won't because I want it to come from your heart. We shall be back to our lives soon. I have waited for ten years, Hazel. I have my needs - please don't make me wait too long."

He released the embrace and turned to leave her house.

"Thank you, Ethan, for the night and for my gift," she managed to say. Ethan nodded and left immediately. His night was made, but he knew he needed to win Hazel's love over, finally.

CHAPTER ELEVEN

Sweet jealousy is the currency of love
Never consuming for destruction
But claiming territories and boundaries.

Hazel heard loud bangs on the door. Still dressed in her evening outfit, she realized she had fallen asleep in the living room. She wondered who was pounding so aggressively. Peering through the spyhole, she saw Richard. When she opened the door, she was taken aback by his expression. His face was twisted in rage, as though he were on fire.

"Richard?" She asked, bewildered by his anger.

Richard paced for a moment before turning to face her. He tried to be calm, but his voice trembled slightly. At this point, he did not care if there were cameras or not in Hazel's house.

"I have always loved you, Hazel. What did I do to deserve this?" He pulled out his phone and showed Hazel pictures of her and Ethan the previous night.

"What were you doing with him, and why were you so close? You lied to me, saying you were going out with a female friend, and I find my fiancée in the arms of a dead man! Really, Hazel? When did you start lying to me?"

Hazel took a deep breath, shocked first by Richard's anger and outburst, and even more by how he had obtained the pictures. She knew he must have been monitoring her.

"Richard, please calm down. Yes, I went out last night, and as you can see, I'm still in my outfit. Eniola, Ethan's sister, is my friend, and it's true she invited me out for dinner, at the time of the invitation, I didn't know it was my birthday, and because I already agreed to meet her, I mentioned it when you wanted to take me out. When I arrived, Ethan was there. He gave me a gift and asked for a dance. That was all. Nothing else happened."

Richard could not reply. He was fuming, pacing back and forth. He eventually sat down, tears rolling down his cheeks, which surprised Hazel. He looked at her repeatedly, unsure if he could still fight for her love. He feared he was losing her to Ethan, who, with his wealth, seemed like a formidable rival.

"Hazel..." he began softly. "I don't doubt your loyalty, but the only way this will stop is if we get married as soon as possible. I don't trust Ethan or anything about him. Yes, he was your husband, but he's dead now, and we don't know what else he'll do to you. I love you, Hazel. Please don't make me question our love and future."

"Come," he said, reaching out to her, but Hazel froze. She realized in that moment that she couldn't postpone her decision any longer. She needed to make up her mind about whom she wanted to be with.

"No Richard, it was my birthday, and I didn't know Ethan would be there. I went out with a friend, and yes, Ethan came and asked for a dance. Should I have refused him? I didn't think much of it, which was why I danced with him."

"So, what will you do about the gift?" Richard asked, closely watching her every move. Shocked that he knew, Hazel lowered her gaze and responded;

"I intentionally left the key on the table at the restaurant. I wasn't going to accept the gift until I was sure of where the three of us stand."

"Three of us? What do you mean, Hazel?"

"I mean me, you and Ethan. I'm caught in between the two of you.

"Hazel, are you saying you are thinking of considering both of us? I thought you knew you wanted me."

"I do, Richard. Remember, I showed up at the wedding. I wanted my life with you, but then Ethan showed up. Please don't make this any harder for me, Richard. I am in this with you."

"Then show me you are for me, Hazel. Show me," Richard replied, looking intently at Hazel.

Hazel was stuck. She let out a heavy sigh, sank into a nearby chair. She became lost in thought for a long time— even long after Richard had stormed out, his presence seemingly forgotten.

****

Very early the next day, Hazel left her house without telling either Richard or Ethan where she was going. She sent each of them a text:

"In solitude. Please don't look for me."

She turned her phone to airplane mode, needing time to seek God's guidance in solitude. She was more confused than ever before and uncertain about whom she should choose. She decided to visit the church where she had been christened, an old Pentecostal church that had always been a place of refuge, hope, restoration, and preservation for her. She loved the childhood teachings she had received there, the families that worshipped there, and the doctrines she grew up with. The church was situated on a hill. It was built over eighty years ago but well-maintained and always looking nice.

She did not inform her parents she was coming and did not want to be recognized, so she wore shades and went straight to the altar to pray, leaving immediately after. She needed space and time to make the most important decision of her life. Both men were fierce and determined, both going to great lengths for her. Ethan had given her a car, and Richard had given her a smart house as birthday gifts. She loved both men in different ways and was troubled, not wanting to make the wrong choice and regret it.

Richard had been the man she was going to marry just a few weeks ago. He had stood by her, bringing life and hope to her. She never imagined a time would come when she would face such a tough decision. Richard had overlooked her situation as a widow and loved her unconditionally. He was her love and hope, loving her dearly. Ethan, on the other hand, had made her who she was, especially in her business. He loved her, cared deeply, and had told her he went to prison because of a common enemy she was yet to know. She suspected it must have been one of the many women who had wanted to marry Ethan.

She checked into a hotel and went to the church's prayer mountain. She had embarked on some fasting too. She was confused and needed clarity of purpose and thoughts.

"Lord, I know you do speak, please speak to me Your perfect will."

She had access to the church as the door was open. She met some women having a prayer meeting. She proceeded to the altar straight; this was day one of her fast. She opened her Bible and read Psalm 121. This was the anchor Scripture she was using for this spiritual connection.

I will lift up my eyes to the hills-- From whence comes my help?

My help comes from the Lord, Who made heaven and earth.

He will not allow your foot to be moved; He who keeps you will not slumber.

Behold, He who keeps Israel Shall neither slumber nor sleep.

The Lord is your keeper; The Lord is your shade at your right hand.

The sun shall not strike you by day, Nor the moon by night.

The Lord shall preserve you from all evil; He shall preserve your soul.

The Lord shall preserve your going out and your coming in From this time forth, and even forevermore.

On the third day, she rose to leave after her prayers when she noticed a frail man entering the church. Though she had been trying to avoid any interactions, she felt compelled to greet him. She offered a polite greeting in the Yoruba traditional manner and turned to go, but the man smiled warmly at her, a broad and friendly smile that caught her off-guard.

"Daughter of Zion…" he said, his smile softening. Hazel, now more surprised, looked at him closely.

"Do I know you, sir?" she asked, forcing a smile, as she tried to place him. She had only greeted him out of respect.

"I'm one of the sanctuary keepers. My name is Ajao. While I was praying a short while ago, the Lord asked me to speak to you from the book of Judges – specifically Judges 6:36-40. I see a fierce battle over you, involving two men. All I can tell you is that God will give you a sign, like the one Gideon asked for. Peace to you." He then knelt down to pray right away, seemingly finished with what he had to say.

"Sir, I came here to pray, to seek the face of the Lord. I was christened in this church, and my parents raised us here. I don't believe I know you, sir, but I'm amazed at your revelations."

"Daughter of Zion, I must pray now. I spoke to you as instructed. May God make the words clearer in your mind. Peace unto you."

"Amen," Hazel replied with a sigh of relief, though still slightly confused. She felt the need to thank God for speaking to her and decided to watch events as they unfolded. When she returned to the hotel where she was staying, she immediately opened her Bible to read the passage the man had mentioned. She turned to Judges 6:36-40 and began to read:

> *So Gideon said to God, "If You will save Israel by my hand as You have said--*
>
> *look, I shall put a fleece of wool on the threshing floor; if there is dew on the fleece only, and it is dry on all the ground, then I shall know that You will save Israel by my hand, as You have said."*

And it was so. When he rose early the next morning and squeezed the fleece together, he wrung the dew out of the fleece, a bowlful of water.

Then Gideon said to God, "Do not be angry with me, but let me speak just once more: Let me test, I pray, just once more with the fleece; let it now be dry only on the fleece, but on all the ground let there be dew."

And God did so that night. It was dry on the fleece only, but there was dew on all the ground.

She whispered a silent prayer, "Lord, just as Gideon asked You to wet the fleece with the dew of heaven, I ask today, even though it's painful, that the one You have not ordained for me will be the one to let go of me by his own free will. Show me a sign that I may choose wisely and carefully whether it be Ethan or Richard. You know they've played significant roles in my life. They both deserve happiness and love, but Lord, show me Your will. I submit to Your will, no matter how hurtful. Let your will prevail, in Jesus' name I pray. Amen."

CHAPTER TWELVE

Clearer His will is shown
For those who will walk with Him
Trust God, even in the dark
A pearl from my ribs I prayed for!

Richard was furious with his private investigators; none had managed to uncover the truth about what happened to Ethan during the ten years of his disappearance. He had spent a fortune trying to unravel the person of Ethan, but the lack of answers only made him more curious and more worried. He had hired another investigator when he was not pleased with the result Jackson brought. He decided to confront Ethan himself. He knew he might be making a risky decision, but his mind was made up. His investigators had pinpointed Ethan's residence, just as Ethan's own investigators knew where Richard lived.

Disguising himself, Richard bypassed all security checks and managed to reach Ethan's house. It was a beautiful mansion sitting on two acres of land. Ethan, relaxing in his private swimming pool, noticed the arrival of an unexpected guest. He instructed his security to let the visitor in, though he remained cautious, considering his traumatic past. As Ethan wrapped a towel around himself and headed inside, he could not shake a strange feeling about the visitor.

"Sir, this gentleman claims to be from Eniola and has urgent information for you," the security man announced. Richard, hidden behind fake beards and glasses, smiled. Ethan, sensing something off, decided to proceed with caution.

"Bring him to the guest living room," Ethan instructed, before slipping through the back door. He quickly called his sister to confirm her safety.

"Who did you send over?" Ethan asked Eniola.

"Hi, bros, me? No one," she replied, puzzled by his question.

"Someone's here saying he is from you. I've got a feeling this is Richard. Life has taught me to sniff out a rat from far off. I'll fill you in later if my hunch is right." He hung up, scrutinizing the security camera footage. After zooming in on the visitor, Ethan's suspicions solidified, though he decided to confirm it himself.

After a quick shower, Ethan dressed comfortably and entered the guest living room. Richard stood as Ethan walked in, their eyes meeting.

"Welcome, Richard. I know you're not from Eniola—I just spoke to my sister. What brings you here?" Ethan's voice was calm, but Richard was taken aback by how easily Ethan had seen through his disguise.

"You can take off the fake beards and dark shades. Please, sit down." A smile played on Ethan's lips, memories of his hardships flashing through his mind. He was not one to be easily deceived anymore. Richard hesitated, then removed his shades and peeled off the fake beard.

"Thank you, Ethan. I apologize for the disguise, but the security around here is tight—almost as tight as mine. I came to talk to you, and I know you weren't expecting me."

"You guessed right, I was not expecting you, what can I do for you?" Ethan asked, noting that Richard too was handsome with his refined appearance and youthful features.

"Ethan, I know you loved Hazel and circumstances tore you apart. Hazel was deeply heartbroken and was willing to give love a second chance, with me. Then you reappeared after ten years. Where were you during those years? I need to know you won't abandon her again if you get her back. Where were you, Ethan?"

Ethan held Richard's gaze for a moment before sipping water from his glass. He paced the room, seeming lost in thought, then turned back.

"Richard, I admire your courage. You love my Hazel very much. Didn't Jackson give you all the information you wanted about me?"

Richard's heart skipped a beat, shocked that Ethan knew about the detective he had hired. How did Ethan know? Suddenly, he felt so small in the presence of Ethan.

"Jackson?" Richard asked, pretending not to remember for a moment.

"Yes, Jackson," Ethan replied with a sly smile.

"I wasn't expecting that. I just want to know where you were for those ten years. Hazel almost died, Ethan."

"I can't tell you that, Richard. But one day, you'll hear my story—when all of God's promises to me are fulfilled. One of those promises is getting my wife back and rebuilding my family. I never intended to hurt Hazel, but I know that's not the real reason you're here, Richard."

Richard was careful, knowing how powerful Ethan had become. He questioned whether coming to see him alone was a wise decision after all.

"Ethan, where were you for a whole of ten years? Why did you suddenly appear on the day Hazel was getting married? How did you know to come to the wedding venue? Was this planned, Ethan?"

"Never, my life without Hazel was not planned that way. Life happened to Hazel and me. It was never planned."

"Please answer my question, Ethan."

"Richard, I didn't plan this, but you should know that I love Hazel. I will fight to get her back. Would you consider stepping down in this battle? Because, trust me, I won't lose Hazel again."

Ethan moved closer, locking eyes with Richard. "I advise you, brother, leave Hazel alone. I showed you one of my scars on the day you wanted to marry her. I've been through life and death. Please, leave Hazel for me. That's the best gift you can give her." Ethan smiled.

Richard observed Ethan, sensing the futility of their conversation. He left Ethan's house and headed to his car. As he drove home, he stopped at a restaurant, deeply troubled by their exchange. Something about the ten-year gap in Ethan's life seemed impossible to uncover, and he wondered how long he could continue fighting for Hazel. He thought about her for a long time, tears streaming down his cheeks. He had never cried over any other woman except Hazel, and this was the second of such instance. Women had always been the ones crying for his love, but Hazel was different. She had become a huge part of his life for the past three years. Everything about Hazel brought him joy and satisfaction. Her simplicity, love, patience, calmness and her care. She was everything he needed. Now he felt he was losing the battle to a stronger opponent. He wished he had married Hazel earlier because something told him he would never marry Hazel now that Ethan was back.

Richard was still shocked that Ethan knew about the private investigator. Where had Ethan been for those ten years? For the first time in his relationship with Hazel, Richard decided to ask for a break. Seeing Ethan had made it clear to him that continuing with Hazel did not make sense. He realized that Ethan loved her deeply, and in time, the truth about those missing years would come out. He recalled seeing Hazel with Ethan on her birthday, how happy and relaxed she was with him. Although she did not know Richard had been watching from a distance, he had noticed a spark in her eyes that he had never seen with him. She seemed to glow with joy in Ethan's presence, and Richard realized that Hazel might truly be the pearl from Ethan's ribs.

He remembered Ethan's piercing words *"Richard, I didn't plan this, but you should know that I love Hazel. I will fight to get her back. Would you consider stepping down in this battle? Because, trust me, I won't lose Hazel again."*

He picked up his phone and sent a text to Hazel:

"My beloved Hazel,

I have fought so hard to keep us together and to make you my wife. I went to see Ethan today, not sure why I decided to, but I realized he is a better fit for you. He will not back off or let go. Please make sure to find out why he disappeared for a whole ten years, as his absence was what brought me into your life. I love you, Hazel, today and forevermore. I pray you find peace and utmost love with Ethan.

Forever,

Richard Akinja.

Richard wept uncontrollably after that. That night, he booked a flight to England. His mother had been right: Hazel needed to be with the man she had married. Ethan's return meant she was no longer free to be with him. Richard knew this love would be hard to replace.

CHAPTER THIRTEEN

The pearl from my ribs
The one I fought for
My joy, my life, my completeness

Hazel was in utter shock when she woke up the next day after praying with Judges 6 the night before in her hotel room. Seeing the text from Richard, she was overwhelmed and wanted to know what had happened and what had influenced his decision. She was not expecting things to change so quickly, and as she shivered, tears began to roll down her cheeks. She did not know whether to be happy or sad. Although an answer had come to her prayers, she felt a deep sadness and cried even more. She remembered the words of the sanctuary keeper, spoken to her just the night before:

I'm one of the sanctuary keepers. My name is Ajao. While I was praying a short while ago, the Lord asked me to speak to you from the book of Judges – specifically Judges 6:36-40. I see a fierce battle over you, involving two men. All I can tell you is that God will give you a sign, like the one Gideon asked for. Peace to you."

Hazel truly was not prepared for that answer that came almost instantly; it felt as if a part of her had been ripped away. However, she also felt a heavy weight lift from her mind, realizing that she would be settling with the husband of her youth, the man who had shaped her into the woman she had become—a successful multimillionaire. That man was none other than Ethan Adebayo!

Hazel felt a deep sorrow for Richard, the man who had made her life meaningful over the past three years. He had loved her truly, and she mourned the end of their relationship as she tried to focus on the present and the future. Despite her sadness, she knew the answer was Ethan. A renewed love for him began to swell in her heart, and she knew she would have to learn to love him all over again. She weighed the thoughts of losing Richard, sweet, patient Richard. He did nothing to deserve this heartbreak, she felt sorry for how things played out. She was torn between these two men and she was almost losing her mind. She knew only a divine intervention would work and she was grateful for getting one.

Briefly, she remembered again the frail man she had seen at the church the previous night; his words had come to fulfilment in her life.

****

Ethan was surprised when he received a text from Hazel. She wanted to see him, which was unexpected, but it filled him with hope. He immediately called her.

"Hazel, dear, I got your text."

"Yes, Ethan, I would like to see you tomorrow."

"Okay," Ethan replied with a smile, sensing that his days of waiting were about to end. "I'll book a table at Français Seul restaurant. I know you love French meals. I'll see you at 7 p.m. tomorrow evening."

Ethan was thrilled by this development. He felt good about it and was ready to let Hazel into a world of secrets—secrets he had tried to share earlier but could not. He looked forward to an evening of bliss and reunion.

****

Ethan looked sharp in his suit, after a quick grooming session. He arrived at the restaurant before Hazel and paid for an exclusive spot reserved for couples. As he waited, Hazel arrived looking stunning in her lavender gown. Her hair was elegantly styled, her makeup simple, and her dress glowed against her dark skin. Her heart skipped a beat when she saw Ethan. She knew her Heavenly Father had endorsed this relationship once again, but she had questions that needed answers.

After placing their orders, Hazel looked at Ethan, her gaze steady and unblinking.

"I want all the truth, every truth, Ethan. What happened in the ten years you were missing? I need to know."

Ethan's smile faded as he looked deeply into Hazel's anxious eyes. He paused for a moment, considering how to begin. He stared at the woman sitting across from him, remembering all the suffering he had endured, and then he began to speak.

"Promise me, Hazel, that you will absorb everything well. I promise I'll tell you everything, but it will break your heart. After that, I hope you'll heal, and we can bond together and be man and wife again."

He sighed deeply, took a sip of juice from his glass, and started slowly.

"Sometimes in our lives, our enemies aren't faraway; they are within and close by." He paused, watching Hazel's face closely.

"When we were courting, I told you your twin sister wanted me so badly. Her lust was out of this world. You dismissed it repeatedly because you trusted and believed in her." Ethan paused again, noting the confusion on Hazel's face as he mentioned her late twin sister. She was clearly wondering why he started with Helen, but she remained silent, ready to listen to everything.

"Your sister was dating powerful men—top military politicians and decision-makers. I was supposed to travel on an official assignment, as you recall, but I had to pick up a few things at the mall. To my surprise, a large number of military officers, along with some police officers, came to the mall to arrest me with a warrant. I asked what I had done, and they said I had to go to the police station to tell my story. This was on April 2nd of that year…" Ethan paused, searching Hazel's face for a reaction.

"I tried to reach you and Lawyer Freewill, but I couldn't. My phones were taken from me. I had no idea what I had done, and no one would tell me. At the police station, I faced the most humiliating time of my life. I was taken to prison without trial, without representation. I met different men in prison and was further transferred to another prison where I was incarcerated. I was injured, maimed, and one of my toes was amputated due to an untreated infection." Ethan's voice shook as he recalled the loss of a part of his body. "It was totally dark in the prison—no light, no exit, no joy. I drank my own urine when there was no food or drink. I suffered without knowing my offense." He noted Hazel's face, her frown deepening as she tried to keep calm.

"The day I was taken away, a plane crash happened. How my name ended up on the manifest was a mystery until much later. The crash wasn't planned but it worked in our enemy's favor to cover up my abduction." Tears began to stream down Ethan's face as he recalled the events. He was not one to cry easily but the details were overwhelming.

"A few days later, Hazel, I had a visitor in prison. Guess who I saw?"

"Who was it?" Hazel asked, her voice trembling.

"Helen."

"What? She knew you were there?" Hazel screamed, her eyes wide with shock.

"No, she didn't just know I was there; she planned everything that happened to me, to us, Hazel. She planned my kidnap. I was meant to rot in prison forever. She used her military connection a lot, including getting my name on the manifest for the plane. That way, I was dead to you forever. She wanted to set me free if I agreed to marry her and leave the country. She was really crazy."

Hazel broke down in tears, unable to believe what she was hearing. Their orders arrived, but Hazel could not eat. She could not stop crying; however she tried. Ethan did not attempt to stop her, much as it hurt, he knew she needed to continue to hear the details.

"Hazel, I went through all this because I was faithful to you. Your twin sister never loved you. She felt she wasn't as lucky as you in marriage, but she didn't wait for her own time. I was shocked to see her and hear all the rubbish she was saying."

"You know she died a year after the supposed plane crash in a motor accident. Oh, Helen, but why?" Hazel sobbed loudly.

Ethan lifted his eyebrow at what Hazel said, looking at her intently.

"No, Hazel, you won't believe what I'm about to tell you. Your sister was more than wicked—she was callous. She had no heart or conscience. Your sister didn't die, Hazel. She just died a month ago."

"What???" Hazel asked in utter disbelief. "No, that's not possible!"

Ethan sighed. "She kept coming once every six months or so during all the times I was incarcerated. She stopped coming about six months ago when the military handed over power to the present civilian government. I and some other inmates who were never tried were all released. She did not know for sure I was freed. Helen seemed to have some psychiatric issues. You heard that she died in an accident about a year after the supposed plane crash, which was untrue. She did what she wanted to do with me because she was hoping I would give in to her, and then we could relocate to another country and start a new life as husband and wife. She wanted you all to think she had died. I hate to tell you this, Hazel, but Helen was a reincarnation of the real devil."

"So, how did she eventually die?" Hazel asked. "This is too much."

"When she eventually found out I had left the prison, she committed suicide. When I got out, I tried to bounce back. Eniola had done so much in my absence; she is a worthy sister. I was able to contact my lawyer and recover

145

a lot of my assets and wealth. Fortunately, my bank is still operational. I had to get back on my feet, but Helen was on the run. All her military backups were arrested, and she no longer had a power base. My guys caught her, but she committed suicide before we could hand her over to the police for prosecution since her men were no longer in power. I had all my plans, and I needed her out of the picture. I have paperwork to show for this, Hazel."

"Please stop..." Hazel pleaded, as she stood up, picked up her purse and headed to her car. The information was too much for her to bear. Ethan walked right behind her. He was not surprised at her reaction, he had prepared for this. He got in the car with her right away. Hazel was crying so much that all her makeup was smeared. She could not drive. Ethan held her; they were facing each other, and Ethan gently stroked her back.

"I'm so sorry, Ethan," she muttered amid sobs. "I am so sorry you went through all of that. Please forgive my sister. She used to have some behavioural issues as a kid, but we thought she outgrew it; we never knew it got worse. Please forgive her, please forgive us. My darling, you went through so much."

Darling? Ethan thought. What happened to Richard?

"I'm so sorry this came as a huge surprise," Ethan replied. "I never meant to hurt you, but your sister tore us apart. She wreaked a lot of havoc. Look at the ten years we've been apart. A lot could have been achieved. It was by a stroke of grace that I knew you were getting married that day, and I had to hire some military troops to come in case something was going to hinder me. I almost died seeing Richard almost make you his bride."

"Oh my God! This is a lot. I had prayed to know God's mind concerning me and either you or Richard, and I never prepared for this. Helen, Helen…aww." Hazel did not know whether to mourn her or be happy she committed suicide.

She started crying again. She remembered the scary dream she had of Helen on the day she was supposed to marry Richard and was admitted to the hospital. Now she had a meaning for the knife and how Helen had stabbed her in the back. She had pondered the dream many times but could not make much of it because she did not know this part of the story. This was beyond revealing. Hazel wondered why Helen did this evil to her, and to think she had just died was terrible.

Hazel wept bitterly. Ethan had to drive her home and they talked along the way. Ethan confessed how he had been monitoring Hazel's house through his cameras. He told her how Richard came to visit him. They were open about everything that had happened. Hazel also told him she and Richard had parted ways. It was a very long night for the two of them. When he parked in front of her house, he turned to her.

"Can I come in tonight?" he asked, his voice full of emotion, and Hazel knew what he meant.

"Not tonight. Let my pastor bless this union again.

It's been a long time for me. We need God's grace for the journey ahead. I have not totally gotten over Richard too. All this is so sudden, one minute I thought I was a widow, went through that harrowing experience at the mental institution, was put on medication and different therapy for a whole year, I get out and years later I met and fall in love with Richard, we had a wedding and then you showed up, I don't understand why I have a lot of twists and turns in my life. I just hope there is an end to all of this." She paused looking and searching Ethan's face.

"Richard truly loved me Ethan, I feel for him, he invested time, his heart and a lot in me." Hazel said reflecting briefly on Richard.

"I understand Hazel. I truly do but your sister brought this on us. Nothing Richard is passing through now in terms of heart break *which you did not intentionally cause* can compare to me being in prison for ten years. I was stabbed, maimed and lost a body part. You were in the mental health hospital and went through a fake widowhood experience. This was a lot for us. I pray Richard finds love and joy in his life." He looks at her intently

"Would you rather go back to him?" Ethan asked searching Hazel's face, he knew she loved him. Hazel looked at him with a smile, she could not afford that.

"No Ethan. I belong to you. I am so sorry for all you went through because of my sister. I am glad you came on time, one more hour and I would have been Richard's wife."

"God has never left me Hazel, He never left us. I promise to always be by your side henceforth. This information cannot be shared with your parents Hazel or you will send them to early grave." Ethan said hoping Hazel will keep all she learned tonight with her. Hazel nods positively.

"I understand"

There was dead silence between them. Each lost in his/ her own thoughts for a while.

"I'm grateful to have you back." Ethan said holding her hands, he had dreamt of this hour for a long time.

"I love you, Hazel Victoria Adebayo." Hazel smiled; the night brought too much information she was processing in her head.

"I love you too," Hazel replied. "I never stopped Ethan. I pray nothing will ever pull us apart."

"Never, my pearl, my jewel" He kissed her forehead and watched her get down from the car back to the house.

****

Ethan was thankful for this beautiful day as he and Hazel walked down the streets of Paris. It had been three months since their formal reunion and blessing. Hazel was eager to share some exciting news with her husband.

"I missed my period," she said to Ethan.

149

Ethan was overjoyed and lifted her up into the air. "What???"

"Yes, honey, we're having our first baby! You're about to be a daddy!" Hazel exclaimed.

Ethan danced with Hazel in his arms, his joy as solid as gold. Hazel truly felt like she was a pearl from Ethan's rib. Everything aligned perfectly with Ethan by her side!

TO GOD BE THE GLORY, GREAT THINGS HE HATH DONE!

July 24th, 2024